C0-DAE-023

Praise for Bestselling Author

SUZANNE FORSTER

"Absolutely delicious."
—*Philadelphia Inquirer*

"Thrillingly suspenseful!"
—*Publishers Weekly*

above her head—and let fly the questions crowding

New York Times and *USA TODAY* bestselling author Suzanne Forster has written over thirty novels and has been the recipient of countless awards, including the National Readers Choice Award. Suzanne has a master's degree in writing popular fiction and teaches and lectures frequently. She lives in Newport Beach, California, and can be contacted through her Web site at www.suzanneforster.com.

SUZANNE FORSTER

Island Heat

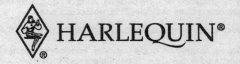

HARLEQUIN®

TORONTO • NEW YORK • LONDON
AMSTERDAM • PARIS • SYDNEY • HAMBURG
STOCKHOLM • ATHENS • TOKYO • MILAN • MADRID
PRAGUE • WARSAW • BUDAPEST • AUCKLAND

ISBN-13: 978-0-373-19870-2
ISBN-10: 0-373-19870-1

ISLAND HEAT

Dear Reader,

Every once in a while an author has a real-life experience that begs to be turned into a story. Sometimes it's a magical place, an extraordinary person, or an unexpected adventure. With *Island Heat* it was all three. The story was inspired by a trip my husband and I took to the island of Barbados in the West Indies—and from the moment we landed at the island's airport, I sensed that we were on the brink of something unusual.

The fun started when we were "kidnapped" by our taxi driver. We gave him the name of our hotel—Sam Lord's Castle—and thought we'd been understood, but two hours into what should have been a half-hour trip, we were still captive in his backseat—moving farther away from civilization. At that point we were no longer certain he was a taxi driver. He didn't seem to understand a word we said, or was pretending not to.

Finally, he stopped at a gas station that also sold food. Inside the store, he spoke in hushed tones with some suspicious-looking characters. Possibly my imagination was working overtime—it's a hazard of writing fiction—but better safe than sorry! We left some money on the seat and made a run for it. As we stole away with our luggage, I knew this would be a scene in a book, and that my heroine would be kidnapped by a taxi driver. I also knew the hero would rescue her. Unless, he'd set the whole thing up!

Enter Lauren Cambridge and Justin Dunne. Lauren is visiting Barbados for the first real vacation of her life, and Justin is there for reasons much more mysterious. What they have in common is a lightning-bolt attraction and their mutual destination, Sam Lord's Castle, a nineteenth-century Georgian mansion that exists to this day. According to local legend, the castle was once the home of Sam Lord, an infamous pirate who stole his bride, Lucy, from her aristocratic English family and brought her to Barbados, where he kept her a prisoner of sensual delights. These are just a few of the delicious elements that I incorporated into *Island Heat*. I hope you enjoy the trip as much as I did!

Suzanne Forster

One

"Who me? Afraid of falling in love?" Lauren Cambridge stopped her pacing long enough to stare at her friend, Rene Browning, and add guardedly, "What's that supposed to mean?"

Rene smiled faintly, settled back into the cordovan comfort of her executive chair and steepled her fingers against her chin.

Lauren resumed pacing. She knew that look. It was the secret weapon that Rene reserved for patients who were avoiding self-examination. Lauren tried reminding herself that she was *not* one of Rene's patients, but it did little to calm her disquiet. In any other setting, she could have ignored the fact that her old college buddy was now a prominent Seattle psychiatrist. But not here. This was Rene's office, her arena, her sanctum sanctorum. Diplomas and certificates lined the walls, an obligatory aquarium sat on the credenza behind her, and pale midmorning sunlight glinted off a desk sign that read Rene Browning, M.D.

Never one to be intimidated, Lauren stopped in her tracks and countered Rene with a look of her own. "Well?" she asked, hands on hips, arching one eyebrow in undeniable question.

Rene grinned. "I don't know how to put it any plainer, Cookie. You are what we in the shrink business call a love phobic. You're scared silly of a meaningful relationship—and always have been, I suspect."

Lauren wondered briefly why her friend had waited all these years to drop this little bombshell on her, but she didn't take the time to ask. She was too busy defending herself against the accusation. "How can you say that, Rene? I've had meaningful relationships." Lauren began counting them off on her fingers. "There was Conrad in high school, Bruce in college. And just last year, Nigel, that redheaded Londoner." She smiled triumphantly. "I almost married him."

"Nigel was more concerned with *his* looks than yours," Rene reminded her, none too subtly. "I wasn't fortunate enough to know Conrad, but Bruce wasn't the last of the red-hot lovers, either, as I remember." She sat forward in her chair, bedside manner forgotten. "Lauren, no matter what you may have told yourself, you weren't emotionally involved with any of those men. You were just going through the motions. They were *safe*."

"And what's wrong with a safe man?"

"Nothing, as long as you're in love with him."

Rene had her there. Lauren glanced at the aquarium. She felt like a hooked goldfish, and instinct told her it was useless to fight. "Uncle," she murmured.

"Okay," Rene said softly, "now we're getting somewhere." She stood up from her desk and went to stand by the window, gazing out for a moment, then turning back to Lauren, her expression expectant. They both knew it was Lauren's move.

Lauren sighed, sinking into the nearest chair. "What am I doing *wrong*, Rene? I'm reasonably attractive, aren't I?" She consulted the aquarium again, seeking her own reflection this time, and was reassured by what she saw—a chic, sensible woman with chestnut hair and blue-gray eyes. "I'm a successful financial analyst. I like men. I work with them, play tennis with them at the club and even date them semiregularly. But what comes of it?" She threw up her hands in despair. "*Nothing.* I'm thirty-three years old, and I've never been in love. Can you believe it? No fireworks, no lightning bolts, nothing!" Glancing down, as though the answer were hidden somewhere in her solar plexus, she murmured, "Do you think it could be glandular?"

Rene shook her head with exaggerated slowness and tapped her forehead.

"It's all in my head?" Lauren questioned. "I'm crazy?"

"Not as in certifiable," Rene assured her, "but you've got an interesting quirk or two." She sat on the narrow windowsill and folded her arms. "You know I'm a firm believer in self-discovery, Lauren. We each have all the answers already—in here and in here," she said, indicating her head and then her heart. "We just need a little help occasionally to tune in, to listen." She paused consideringly. "I make it a rule never to offer instant insight, but in your case I'm tempted."

"Don't stop now," Lauren prompted.

Rene took a preparatory breath. "Okay—to get specific, you've been playing a game that some of us in the profession call Blemish. It's a common defense against emotional involvement. Everybody does it now and then. But you, my friend, have elevated it to an art form. At the tender age of thirty-three, Lauren Cambridge is headed for the Blemish Hall of Fame—"

"I never liked games much, Rene," Lauren cut in. "Especially games that sound like skin conditions."

"Shall I go on?"

Lauren glanced at the ceiling in mock despair. "Try and stop her."

"Have you ever noticed what happens when you find a man attractive?" Amused sympathy warmed Rene's brown eyes. "I have—countless times. You zap him. You search out a defect, real or imagined, and he's *history*, disqualified before anything can happen. That's Blemish. It's the way you protect yourself from the possibility of emotional pain—rejection, abandonment, whatever it is you're afraid of."

Lauren lifted her eyebrows skeptically. "Why should I do that? I've had a rejection or two, sure, but it's not like I'm one of the walking wounded. And I've certainly never been abandoned—" Her friend's expression stopped her. "I have? When?"

Rene hesitated, almost sighed. "Your father, Lauren."

"Oh, yeah," Lauren admitted, sobering. "But that's not the same thing. I was five years old, a child."

"What better time to form an opinion about men? A five-year-old girl is impressionable, vulnerable, ready to idolize any father figure who'll hold still long enough. Yours didn't. He took off and left you and your mother holding the bag, not once, but several times if I remember correctly."

Lauren nodded, recalling the tall, wheat-haired man who'd twirled her in his arms and called her Butterfly. Her father was a handsome drifter, a long, lanky shadow of a man. "She divorced him when I was seven," Lauren remembered aloud. "But by then it was too late. She was angry and embittered. He'd turned her against men."

"And between the two of them," Rene observed quietly, "they turned *you* against men, as well."

Lauren wasn't listening. She was reliving the dire warnings of her childhood. *Alley cats, all of 'em,* her mother had insisted, *with no more morals or character than a rutting stag. And women, damn fools that we are, we don't listen to our own instincts. If we did, we'd never let the devils near us.*

Remembering her mother's rancor as if it were yesterday, Lauren sighed with a bittersweet sound, like laughter, only tainted by sadness. When she looked up, she saw the empathy in Rene's eyes.

"She sure did a job on you," Rene said softly. "I figured as much."

"I suppose she *did* scare me," Lauren said, her throat oddly tight, "but I knew all men weren't like that. And even if I didn't know it then, I certainly know it now."

Rene sat forward. "Of course you know it on a rational level, but emotionally you're still reacting to those childhood messages. We all do, Lauren. It's the way we're made. There's intellect and there's emotion, and the two levels don't always mesh. That's what makes us complex and interesting."

"And crazy?" Lauren sighed.

"A little crazy," Rene conceded.

Lauren rubbed her thumb back and forth along the nubby fabric of the chair arm and wished she didn't suddenly feel so uneasy and so exposed. Over the years she and Rene had often talked about love and sex and all the things women friends talk about, but Rene had never offered a clinical opinion before. And it had never occurred to Lauren to ask for one—or that Rene might know things about her she didn't know herself. She almost wished she hadn't called Rene last night—at two in the morning, actually—in a fit of desperation. *"Rene,"* she'd blurted into the phone, "I just had the god-awfulest nightmare. I was this bag lady in the park. You know, homeless, childless, whiskers on my chin—"

"That's wonderful, Lauren," Rene had drowsily mumbled. "Drop by my office at ten. I've got a free hour."

Lauren had done just that. And here she sat, with her troubled psyche laid bare for Rene and all the world to see.

Rene broke into her musings. "Lauren, you know how much I value our friendship. If I've overstepped—"

"No…it's just that—" Lauren looked up, saw her friend's concern and winked to reassure her that everything was okay. "You must have wanted to tell me this before. Why didn't you?"

Rene winked back. "You never asked."

In that moment Lauren had a glimmer of how complicated it must be for Rene, juggling professional opinions and friendly advice. A psychiatrist's words, however casual, carried with them the implied wisdom of all those years of training and clinical practice. You couldn't offer suggestions casually, even to troubled friends. You had to wait to be asked. Lauren didn't envy Rene that aspect of her life.

A sigh welled up in her chest. But she *did* envy her friend's love life, her marvelous ten-year marriage. Rene had always known her own mind where men were concerned. "Well, what now?" Lauren asked, smiling ruefully. "Around-the-clock therapy until I'm safe to be on the streets again?"

"I had something a little different in mind," Rene said, looking entirely too pleased with herself. "Just say no if you don't like the idea. There's this guy. He's a friend of Ted's—"

"No!" Lauren was out of the chair like a shot. "You know how I feel about blind dates."

"Sorry." Rene held up her hands in a placating gesture. "Scratch Plan A. He's a fascinating man, but probably a little too wild for you, anyway."

Lauren knew bait when she smelled it, but she wasn't biting this time, thank you very much. Gathering up her purse, she decided an exit was in order.

"You're not leaving?" Rene protested. "We haven't discussed Plan B yet."

Eyes narrowed, Lauren measured the aquarium for size. "Does it include drowning a pushy psychiatrist? What would they call that? Shrinkicide?"

"Plan B is a nice, long vacation."

Lauren managed a pained grin. "You're not serious?"

"Why not? You haven't taken one in years." Rene opened her arms expansively. "I'll even give you the name of my travel agent—she's *always* exclaiming the virtues of Barbados. Open up to life, to love. Take some risks, Lauren. And for heaven's sake, if you meet a man you find attractive, give him a chance!" She walked to her desk, scribbled something on her prescription pad, tore it off and handed it to Lauren with a flourish.

To be taken immediately: one fabulous getaway vacation to some exotic port where the men still wear loincloths and beat their chests.

Lauren glanced at it, just the slightest spark of interest in her skeptical smile. "I've never been much good at vacations."

"So you'll get good—with vacations *and* men. Think of it as on-the-job training, an apprenticeship in romance. That should appeal to your workaholic nature."

Romance? Lauren felt a curl of anxiety in her stomach. She tucked the prescription in her purse. "Maybe next summer."

"No—now, Lauren. You're in your prime, but the clock is ticking."

Lauren pursed her lips. How could she take a vacation now? Who would run her investment counseling business while she was gone? Who would water her plants? Or feed her cat, Burger King? No, it was out of the question. There were a million reasons she couldn't break away right now. She exhaled, glad to have the issue resolved so quickly. And yet, in the background of her thoughts, she heard Rene's voice gently urging her on.... *Loosen up, Lauren, have some fun, take some risks. Live, Lauren, live!*

Am I having fun yet? Lauren wondered, sagging to a stop in the middle of the Barbados International Airport terminal. At ten in the morning, the island was already oppressively hot and muggy. Springtime in the tropics indeed, she thought, remembering the travel agent's enthusiasm. If it was May now, the entire Caribbean must be a sauna bath by midsummer.

She dropped her suitcases and shrugged off her garment bag, wondering if she had the wherewithal to hail a taxi. Fifteen straight hours of travel, including connecting flights, layovers, headwinds and an emergency stop in Antigua to refuel had pretty much confirmed her theory about vacations. They'll kill ya!

As she drooped down onto one of the suitcases, a rumbling sound from behind drew her attention. A herd of frazzled tourists, just released from customs, was bearing down on her in a frantic rush to get to the taxi stand outside the terminal.

"You've got two choices, Lauren," she muttered. "Stand your ground and get trampled—or beat 'em to the exits."

She struggled to her feet, dragging suitcases and garment bag along with her. She was halfway there when the horde caught her—jolting her along with them for a few steps and then discarding her in the same way a rambunctious litter of kittens would discard the runt.

"Barbarians," she muttered, watching them swarm the taxis like locusts. By the time she made it outside there was only one taxi left, and she could see immediately why no one had taken it.

The car was an old English Rover that had seen better days. At least two of the windows were broken, the bumpers were dangling like Christmas decorations and what remained of the chassis looked as if it was held together by mud, rust, spit and a lot of faith.

The driver, an elderly Barbadian—or Bajan as the travel brochures had indicated—gave Lauren a hopeful nod. "Tahxee?" he said, waving her over, his gold inlays glinting in the sunlight.

"No, thanks," Lauren demurred politely. "I'll just… wait."

"Come on, come on, tahxee," he insisted, ambling over to pick up her bags. He had the two suitcases and was trying to wrest the garment bag from Lauren's grip when she saw another car roaring up. "Wait!" she cried, tugging back. "Hold it! That must be my ride," she fibbed frantically. "Yes, the hotel's sent a car for me."

Undaunted, he dragged her, the garment bag and the suitcases right along with him. Amazing, she thought, skidding on her heels toward his car. He has the strength of ten men.

"I take you hotel," he chirped, regaling her with a clipped, rapid-fire mixture of English and Bajan—not one word of which she understood. And then he bludgeoned open the jammed trunk of the car and threw her suitcases inside.

"No," she snapped, releasing the garment bag to make a dive for the suitcases. "Thank you, but *no*!" She had the weekender halfway out of the trunk before he slammed down the lid, strangling her brand-new luggage and the resort wear inside. "Will you stop that!" she yelped.

He had the decency to look contrite then—and slightly perplexed. Lauren felt almost guilty as she heaved open the trunk and wrested the bags out. Perhaps he'd misunderstood her. "Thank you, anyway, but I already have transportation," she explained, pointing vaguely toward the car that had driven up and was idling at the curb some twenty feet behind them. It was another taxi, she realized, too preoccupied to care as the bearded driver stuck his head out the window and grinned salaciously at her. All she wanted at the moment was to extricate herself and her luggage from this gung ho cabbie.

By the time she had her bags clear, the driver of the second taxi was standing outside his car with the passenger door open. One good look at him and Lauren instantly regretted her decision. He was razor-thin, with a jagged scar that sealed off his right eye, and a leering smile. A white slave trader if ever I saw one, Lauren thought, turning back to the first taxi driver and smiling wanly. "That offer still good?"

Five minutes later Lauren was lurching away from the terminal in the back seat of the Rover.

"I'm staying at Sam Lord's Castle," she called out over the grunts and groans of the Rover's engine. "Name's Lauren Cambridge. What's yours?" She'd learned in her business that establishing a first-name basis personalized things a little. And also that identifying oneself carried with it a certain responsibility for one's actions.

"Duncan," her driver said, smiling into the rearview mirror.

Lauren smiled back, reassured.

She shouldn't have been. Duncan apparently didn't care one whit about having identified himself. The man was a demon unleashed behind the wheel, and the trip to Sam Lord's promised to be the wildest ride of Lauren's life.

The narrow dirt road corkscrewed through the countryside, zigzagging around hairpin turns and blind corners. Like clockwork, buses bulging with islanders materialized at every turn. And like clockwork, Lauren shrieked out warnings that Duncan blithely ignored. He took perverse delight in playing vehicular "chicken" with everything in his path. Buses, taxis and pedestrians alike dived for the ditches to avoid him.

Only the cows and goats loitering on the straightaways were too stubborn—or too stupid—to move as the Rover bore down on them. Duncan honked and cursed and occasionally sideswiped one of the beasts, which invariably dented the car and left the animal unscathed. Now Lauren understood the Rover's pathetic condition.

Throughout the ride, Lauren's body was paralyzed in a defensive crouch, her knuckles permanently white from clutching at the armrest. She could have sworn she'd seen Hollywood car chases with less action! As Duncan barreled down a side road and swung onto a jutted path, she closed her eyes in a silent plea for deliverance. If I make it through this, she vowed, I'll never take another vacation.

The car hit a bump and sailed into the air. Lauren's eyes flew open. "Duncan," she croaked as they bottomed out briefly and chugged on down the road, "how long till we get there?" She just knew her teeth would still be rattling in her head come Christmas.

"Soon," he promised.

"Soon? Are you sure?" We're going to make it, she realized, clutching her free hand to her chest. *We're going to make it.*

She'd just taken a breath and settled back in the seat

when Duncan hit the brakes and sent the taxi into a squealing, tire-shredding skid.

"What is it?" Lauren gasped. "Are we there?"

The car came to a dead stop and died, its ancient frame shimmying and groaning like a belly dancer past her prime. Fine golden dust exploded in every direction, sparkling magically as the sun hit it. Limp with shock, Lauren gripped the front seat to steady herself. Where were they? Why had Duncan stopped?

It was several seconds before the dust cleared enough to give her an answer. "What is that?" she murmured to the back of Duncan's silent head. "And who is *he*?"

A man stood in front of the taxi. Surrounded by a golden haze, he looked as though he'd stopped the car with his body. Lauren fell silent, questions dying on her lips as the man walked around to Duncan's open window, his white-gold hair glinting in the sunlight.

"My jeep broke down," he said, his voice as textured and grainy-soft as the pale dust coating his arms. "If you're headed for Sam Lord's Castle, mind if I hitch a ride?"

Duncan shook his head. "Sorry. Tahxee full up." With a nervous jerk he twisted the ignition key, and the car coughed and sputtered awake like Rip Van Winkle coming out of his twenty-year sleep.

"Duncan——" Lauren reached out to stay his hand as he shifted the car into low gear. "It's all right."

The Bajan jerked around, obviously startled.

Lauren was surprised at the apprehension in his eyes. It was as though he knew this man——or knew of him.

"It's all right, Duncan," she insisted softly. "Let him ride with us."

"Hey, thanks," the man said, bending down to glance in at Lauren.

It was her first real look at him, and his at her. In the brief moment that their eyes held, Lauren was aware of translucent blue irises, coppery, sunburned skin and a subtly carved mouth. The last detail her mind registered was his mustache, as gold and sun-streaked as his hair.

He was gone from the window several seconds before Lauren realized it. The image of his face held like a snapshot in her mind. Not so much his eyes, she realized, vibrantly blue as they were, but his mouth... hard and yet sensually full-lipped for a man. Yes, it must have been his mouth that made her stomach feel so hollow.

Lauren sat back in the seat, watching him as he brushed himself off before getting in the car. All she could see of him now was his torso, and the dust swirling around him made her think of a great golden dog shaking itself after a swim. He was a big man, she realized, not heavyset, but large-boned and solidly muscled.

All the while he was out there, she was absently aware of a tingle of anxiety in her throat. But it wasn't until he opened the door and slid in beside her that she fully registered what she'd done. It occurred to her that she might still be in a state of shock from her several recent brushes with death. How else could she rationalize offering a ride to a strange man in a strange place? Lauren Cambridge didn't pick up hitchhikers. Especially hitchhikers who threw themselves in front of cars!

"I really appreciate this," he said, his smile revealing a flash of even white teeth.

Lauren smiled back, feeling the tightness in her own facial muscles as she watched him brush a sprinkle of dust from his knee. His khaki shorts revealed bronze legs covered with downy blond hair. Amazingly long, sinewy and nearly naked legs, Lauren observed, her stomach beginning to float again. Her head began to float, as well, and light-headedness wasn't a feeling she was on an intimate basis with—or wanted to be.

"Thanks for the ride," he said again, as though he weren't sure she'd heard him the first time.

She hadn't. "No problem—glad to help."

Duncan shifted the car into gear again, and Lauren settled back into the seat as the Rover pulled away. She felt distinctly uneasy, with a vague sense of something she had absolutely no control over beginning to take shape. The premonition, if that's what it was, was outside of Lauren's sphere of experience. Almost more an intuitive glimmer than a physical sensation, it riveted her attention for a second…and then it disappeared.

Aware that she was functioning on precious little sleep and a lot of nervous energy, Lauren fixed her eyes on the road ahead, mentally preparing herself for the carnival ride that Duncan was about to take them on.

But Duncan had apparently satisfied his thirst for thrills, and his driving was remarkably subdued for the remainder of the trip. Lauren marveled silently as he actually slowed down at the curves and honked his horn to alert pedestrians instead of bullying them off the road.

Was it the hitchhiker who'd put Duncan on his best behavior? Lauren wondered. If so, he seemed to be having a strange effect on everybody in the car.

For the next mile or so, the man next to Lauren was remarkably quiet, and she wondered if she ought to initiate some conversation. But she didn't. She knew she wasn't acting in character at all. This wasn't the Lauren Cambridge she knew, the shrewd and smoothly professional investment counselor who daily charmed and finagled the toughest of customers into availing themselves of her financial services. That Lauren Cambridge would have had this guy's vital statistics and his net worth within the first five minutes. Subtly, of course, and without his ever realizing he'd given her the information. That woman could charm the skin off a mink. All *this* woman could do was manage furtive glances at him.

It was his silence that particularly intrigued her. It almost seemed an invitation to create a personal history for him. The khaki shorts and shirt he was wearing— with his sleeves rolled up above his elbows and the red bandanna loosely knotted around his neck—put her in mind of an African safari guide. The great white hunter, she thought, entertaining a brief reverie of him trekking the savannas of Africa, stalking wild game. It was a wildly romantic notion, and not the only one by far. His sculpted mouth, sun-swept hair and mustache recalled the outlaws of the wild West. In fact, if it wasn't for the safari outfit, she would have sworn she was sharing a taxi with the Sundance Kid.

I'm fantasizing, she realized with a start. Is this what happens to thirty-three-year-old workaholics who've never known love? Full-blown, multiple fantasies in broad daylight?

"They say the castle is haunted. Is that why you picked it?"

Lauren jumped at the sound of his voice. He was waiting for an answer, but it was such a pregnant question she wasn't sure how to respond. "Haunted? Is it really? I didn't know…"

He didn't answer, and finally, to break the silence, she added, "The castle was my travel agent's idea. She booked the entire trip for me—hotel reservations, tours, everything. I'm kind of a novice at vacations."

"A novice?" He smiled mysteriously. "And you chose Barbados? Interesting. You'll learn fast here."

"I will…?" She was finding it impossible to converse with him at her normal conversational pace. Mainly because he never said the expected thing. "Apparently you're familiar with the island," she ventured. "Do you live here?"

"No…" The word trailed off into silence as he turned away to look out the window on his side.

That's it? Lauren thought. Just no? She wasn't used to one-word sentences, and this one felt like a cliff-hanger, as though there were a whole lifetime of information stored up in that one syllable.

"I've got some people to see," he said, turning back to her, "some business to take care of." He exhaled slowly, brushed at something on the seat between them and finally smiled. "Actually, it's business *and* pleasure. I sailed in from Trinidad for the Cockspur Rum Sailing Regatta. My boat's moored at the marina in Bridgetown."

This is a strange man, Lauren decided immediately. Wickedly attractive but strange. She was mentally relegating him to the also-rans when Rene's words gently chided her. *For heaven's sake, if you meet an attractive man, Lauren, give him a chance.*

Another silence fell around them, and this time Lauren took the cue. He didn't want to talk anymore. So be it, she thought, concentrating on their journey and wondering why it was taking so long. At least Duncan's restraint made it possible to see the countryside as more than a blur out the window.

Sam Lord's was on the wind-whipped Atlantic side of the island, and their trip alternated between rolling plains with an occasional palm bent nearly horizontal, and thick, tall fields of green sugarcane.

Clusters of schoolchildren walked along the roadside, their neat blue-plaid uniforms a fascinating contrast to the Bajan women wrapped in colorful prints and balancing huge bundles of sugarcane on their heads.

A sparkle of light drew Lauren's attention back to the man beside her. He held a small object in the palm of his hand, rubbed it with his thumb for a moment and then held it up to the sunlight that flashed through the car window.

It was an uncut stone, grayish in color, and not particularly striking in any way that Lauren could discern. Still, he seemed totally preoccupied with it. She wanted to ask him what it was, but she sensed it would be an intrusion. Instead, she watched the play of the muscles in his forearm as he turned the stone in the light. A workman's arms, she decided, strong and roped with muscle, deeply suntanned from continuous exposure to the elements. This was a man who earned his living out-of-doors, by the sweat of his brow, probably.

There I go again, she thought. Romanticizing. Brushing a damp strand of hair off her forehead, she smiled ruefully and decided the muggy heat must be getting to her. Not to mention jet lag, culture shock and simple exhaustion. Romanticizing? It was a wonder she wasn't hallucinating. After this vacation, she would need a nice long stay in a convalescent home.

"Sam Lord's Castle," Duncan announced.

Lauren looked up as the Rover jolted and bounced to a stop. A Bajan driver and his donkey cart were stalled in the road directly in front of the arched entrance to the resort.

"Move dat ting!" Duncan bellowed, leaning out the window and banging the side of the car. The donkey brayed back, twitched its tail and sat down. Muttering curses, Duncan slammed out of the taxi and went to deal with the situation personally.

Lauren laughed, turned to the hitchhiker and found

him staring at her curiously. Golden sunlight flooded through the car's back window, enveloping them both.

She was caught there for a moment, in the sunlight, in his eyes. "What is it?" she finally managed to whisper.

He didn't seem to have heard her, for it took a while for him to speak. "It's your eyes."

She brought her fingers to her face.

"The color," he said. "I've only seen it one other time."

His intensity startled her, and though Lauren had never been shy in her life, she averted her eyes out of sheer self-consciousness.

He caught her face and drew it back, framing her throat with his fingers. "I'm sorry," he said, his voice an irresistible shimmer of husky, low laughter. "I know I must be embarrassing you. It's just that the color—"

"Color? My eyes are gray."

"*Blue-gray*, like water sapphires." He released her then, exhaling a sound that might have been laughter but held little mirth. "Sorry, I—"

"No, it's all right," she said, taking a long breath.

She thought it *was* all right, but when she looked at him again, her breathing faltered. It was almost painful meeting his eyes. Even though he wasn't touching her, something uncanny was happening inside her, a curling sensation deep in her belly. She wanted to look away. She didn't.

And he didn't, either.

Surrounded by silence and sunlight, they acknowl-

edged each other. There were no words or easy expla-
nations for what was happening, just the exquisitely
silent communication of their senses. They were caught
again, just as before. Nothing needed to be said.
Nothing could be said.

When his gaze drifted almost imperceptibly to her
mouth, Lauren found her eyes darting to his mouth, too.
Vividly, she imagined what was going to happen next—
the touch, the kiss—and her anticipation was heart-
catching. Warmth spread through her like a fire,
weakening limbs, priming nerves. Instinctively, she
tightened against the sensations, trying to hold them
back. Again, she had that glimmer of forces beyond her
control, of something unalterable taking place.

What she didn't realize, couldn't have known with
her limited experience, was that holding back would
heighten every emotion, every sensation…that restraint
was a kind of aphrodisiac. What she *did* know on some
primitive level was that all he had to do was touch her
again and she would unravel like silk.

When he did touch her again, tracing his finger along
the sensitive rise of her cheekbone, she felt as though
tiny firecrackers were bursting inside her, soft and
white, showering sparks like pinwheels. A gasp swelled
in her throat.

She caught his hand and drew back.

Suddenly Duncan was back and the Rover was
jolting forward. As Lauren looked up they were driving
through the arched gateway, past a cluster of expensive
shops on the right and a landscaped courtyard on the left.

They rounded a curve, and the castle came into view, a graceful two-story Georgian mansion with verandas of blue-and-white marble.

"It's lovely," Lauren said as Duncan pulled the car up to the entrance and a tall, dusky-skinned majordomo opened the door for her. Behind him were two flights of marble steps leading into the castle.

Several things pulled at Lauren's attention at once. She was aware of the majordomo waiting for her, Duncan unloading her luggage from the trunk, and the hitchhiker getting out of the car.

"Wait," she said, but he was already walking away.

She scrambled out of her side, oblivious of the men attending her, and called after him. "Where are you going? Are you staying at the castle? What's your name?"

She thought he wasn't going to turn back. In the seconds she waited, his face flashed into her mind, a vivid portrait of bronze and blue and gold.

"Justin," he said, his back to her. He wheeled around, staring hard. She wanted him to smile at her, to reassure her of something, she didn't know what. But he didn't. "Justin…is that all?" she asked.

"What more do you want?" he asked. "A last name? How about Dunne? Will that do?" His eyes flirted with a smile.

As he turned and walked away, she murmured, "Yes, that'll do just fine."

Two

Lauren stood at the foot of the canopied bed in her room and released a sigh mingled with exhaustion and delight. The bedroom, tucked into the southeastern-most corner of the castle on the second floor, was charming. Period-decorated with hand-carved mahogany furniture and English antiques, and accented with fresh-cut flowers in porcelain vases, it brought to mind an Impressionistic tableau by Monet.

She appreciated the room all the more for the trouble her travel agent had gone to to secure the reservation. The resort was a seventy-one-acre complex sprinkled with bungalows, but the castle itself had only ten bedrooms. Luckily, a last-minute cancellation had made this one available.

As she turned, a mirror on the wall adjacent to the

bed caught her eye. Framed in elaborate mahogany scrollwork, it had a carved monkey's head at the top, with glass eyes as green as emeralds. The woodwork was impressive, but the simian features were somehow sinister—the monkey's eyes seemed to follow her as she moved. Lauren quelled a shiver and looked away.

Dismissing the reaction as traveler's nerves, she sat on the bed, removed her shoes and wiggled her cramped toes. She'd read a little about the castle in the brochures the travel agent had supplied her with. She knew it was originally the home of an Englishman named Sam Lord, allegedly a gentleman pirate who hung lanterns on the banyan trees, luring unsuspecting ships onto the reefs in order to loot them.

An enterprising man, Sam Lord, she thought ironically. And apparently a bit of a rake, too. History had it that he'd all but kidnapped a smitten young Englishwoman named Lucy Wightwick, married her against her father's wishes and brought her to the island. When Lucy tired of Sam's rakehell ways and tried to return to England, he'd imprisoned her in the dungeon of this very castle. The brochure hadn't mentioned how Sam and Lucy's story ended, but Lauren doubted it was happy.

Looking around the breezy, sunlit chamber, she couldn't escape the feeling that she'd stepped back in time. The castle's richly textured history emanated from the walls and the furnishings as though the past and its people were something alive, breathing the same air she was. Smiling, she realized she wouldn't have been surprised to see Lucy Wightwick open the door and walk right in.

Lauren had heard of déjà vu experiences, but this was somehow different. As she walked to the window, she had the oddest feeling that the room was responding to her, perhaps even…waiting for her.

Another slight shudder passed through her but was soon forgotten as she lifted the sheer curtain and took in the view. Patchworked with lush gardens and studded with fountains, the vast estate swirled like a rich green blanket toward cliffs on the north and a glorious white sand beach on the south.

It was magnificent.

Lauren remained transfixed at the open window for some time, letting the trade winds caress her face, their warmth heavy with the scent of frangipani and jasmine. In the near distance, melting out of a royal blue horizon, the ocean's turquoise crests and white surf created a delicate silvery lacework. No wonder they call this a paradise, she thought. It was almost more beauty than the eye and the heart could deal with at one time.

Turning away from the window, she was surprised at how refreshed and energized she felt when she should have been exhausted. Her bags waited to be unpacked, but she couldn't bring herself to do it. She was restless, as though there was somewhere she was supposed to be going, something she should be doing. Her travel agent had booked her on various tours but had left today free, apparently thinking Lauren would need to recuperate from the rigors of the trip.

"Free time," Lauren observed, knowing herself all too well, "is murder on the Type A nervous system." An entire afternoon and evening to kill would have been a disquieting prospect even if she hadn't been alone and in an unfamiliar place. Immediately, her mind seized on the most obvious solution. You're in the Caribbean, Lauren, go lie on the beach.

"An isolated section of beach," she amended ten minutes later, frowning at her reflection in the wardrobe mirror. The slinky, white, one-piece swimsuit Rene had convinced her to buy on a prevacation shopping trip was more revealing than she remembered. She wouldn't be doing a lot of swimming in this thing—the papery silk fabric made her wonder if the designer had intended the suit to be disposable.

Much to Lauren's relief, the beach traffic was light that afternoon. Besides the occasional vendor selling shell jewelry and beachwear, there were only a few couples—vacationers so involved with each other, they could have tripped over Lauren and not noticed her.

She scanned the beach for any sign of her multiple-fantasy figure. Vaguely disappointed when she didn't find him, she glanced down at herself and decided to sunbathe on her stomach in case he happened to show up.

After an hour in the sun and two planter's punches, both Lauren's basal temperature and her courage were up, and she brazenly rolled over onto her back.

Glossy with several applications of sunscreen, she stared up at the graceful fronds of the palm swaying above her head—and let fly the questions crowding her mind. Justin Dunne? Who was he? Where had he come from? And where had he disappeared to this morning? He hadn't come into the castle to register, so she could only assume that he was already registered and staying in one of the bungalows on the estate grounds. The thriving hotel chain that had developed the acreage surrounding the castle had been careful to preserve the rugged, sweeping beauty of the eastern coast, and the result was a luxury playground for tourists, complete with restaurants, tennis courts and swimming pools.

Propping herself on her elbows, Lauren scanned the curved beach and marveled at the nervousness she felt just at the thought that she might spot him. Two weeks ago in Rene's office she'd admitted to never having experienced fireworks. This morning she'd felt her first— what? Roman candle? Not an entire Fourth of July display perhaps, but it was a start. Given that the man had barely touched her, she considered it real progress. Rene would be proud.

On that thought, Lauren quelled her instinctive fears about Justin Dunne and the million other questions working in her mind. She was determined to loosen up, to be open to new experiences on this vacation. The old Lauren would have been heading for the exits by now. The new Lauren? Well, she wasn't sure, but she wanted to give her a chance.

By that evening Lauren's enthusiasm had dimmed a little. She ate dinner alone at The Wanderer, a lovely open-air restaurant on the grounds. The fresh vegetable salad and spicy pepperpot soup were delicious, but surrounded by rapt couples at candlelit tables, Lauren was about as uncomfortable as she'd ever been in her life. She felt like a pigeon trapped in an aviary of lovebirds.

Everywhere she looked there were mooning twosomes gazing at each other over their lemon-broiled flying fish and rubbing knees under the tables. My travel agent has booked me into a lovers' hideaway, Lauren thought, despairing. Other than the waiters there didn't seem to be an unattached male in sight.

As Lauren picked over her dessert, she was struck by the irony of the situation. Just when she was ready to take risks, to be open and spontaneous, there was no one to be spontaneous with! The first man who'd aroused her interest in years had done a disappearing act, and the disappointment was enough to have her considering switching resorts.

Back in her room Lauren picked up a steamy romance novel she'd packed for inspiration, and settled into the chair for an evening of reading. She hadn't finished two pages before her mind was registering the low, sensual rhythms of exotic drumbeats drifting through the window behind her. Calypso music. The metallic shimmer of steel drums and a female singer's bluesy voice blended in. As the music picked up pace and volume, Lauren set her book down. Should I? she wondered.

Fifteen minutes later, wearing a crimson halter-top sundress, she was sitting at a corner table in the Main Brace Bar and Lounge, a popular nightspot at the resort, and sipping a foamy greenish drink with spears of pine-apple, sprigs of mint and a name so elaborate she'd already forgotten it. Zombie Fogcutter Mint Fizz or some such thing. Ignoring the entwined couples on the dance floor, she concentrated instead on the steel-drum band with their yellow and black polka-dot shirts and their pulsating music.

One hour and a second Fizz later, the combination of sultry music, steamy heat and clinging, hip-swinging dancers had infected Lauren's brain. This was a mistake. *Okay, Rene, where are all those real men in loincloths?*

The answer came immediately and in physical form.

Men. In droves. Swarming into the Main Brace.

Now I really *am* hallucinating, Lauren thought, watching them pour through the door, line up at the bar and fill up all the available tables. They weren't wearing loincloths—most of them had on business suits—but they were of the male gender, all right. Loud, noisy fellows, clapping one another on the back.

A convention, she realized, averting her eyes as one of them spotted her. When she glanced back, he was headed her way, two drinks in his hand. Lauren squelched the impulse to flee. No, she wouldn't run. She was opening up to new experiences, and this certainly promised to be one.

"Howdy," he called, still several feet away and working his way toward her.

She smiled dutifully—and then gasped as he tripped and plummeted forward. He caught himself but couldn't seem to slow his momentum. Lauren screamed and sprang to her feet as he stumbled, doubled over the table, plopped the drinks down and fell into a chair.

"Are you all right?" she gasped.

"Sure," he assured her, waving her back. "Sit down, sit down." As she did, he winked and pushed the drink toward her. "Great, huh? That was my Gerald Ford imitation."

"*What?* You didn't trip?"

"Oh, hell no," he said, picking up his own drink to toast her. "I've got a million of 'em. Wanna see Bette Davis?"

"No—" Lauren's hand shot up, but he was already pursing his lips, raising his eyebrows and crossing his legs.

"Wot a *dump.*"

He fell back in the chair, grinning like a sweepstakes winner. "Great, huh? Have I got her down or what?"

"Or what," Lauren agreed quickly, afraid she would set him off again. "What's going on?" she asked, looking around the room. "A convention of comedians?"

"No, no," he snorted impatiently. "Vacuum cleaner salesmen. You've heard of Deeper Sweeper, of course. We're this year's top salesmen. Name's Buzz," he announced, grabbing her hand and shaking it vigorously. "They call me Buzzbomb. I outsold last year's high-point man by sixteen uprights and forty-two canisters."

"That's…wonderful." Lauren was smiling, but she couldn't help remembering the Chinese curse about getting what you wished for. And you *had* to wish for men, Lauren, she thought.

Buzz had settled back into his chair and was surveying her with all the smugness of a man who's reached the top of the heap. He picked up his glass and rolled it around, letting the ice cubes clink. "You look like a woman who appreciates fine equipment," he said, unable to conceal his pride, "and I just happen to have some. I've got a Deeper Sweeper of the canister variety up in my room right now. What say? You wanna come on up and have a look at my big, mean cleaning machine?"

Lauren couldn't get her mouth shut, much less answer him.

Undaunted, he leaned forward conspiratorially. "Say…haven't you met me somewhere before? Detroit? The Maui Conference last year?"

"No, *no*," Lauren gasped, "I'm sure of it, Buzz. We've never met."

"Yeah," he said, grinning, "I guess you would've remembered."

"Oh, yes…definitely."

Buzz swung around to check out the dance floor. "Bet you're a fine little dancer," he said, turning back.

"The Rumba Queen of King County."

Where did *that* come from? Lauren wondered, shaking her head in denial. "I didn't say that. I didn't *mean* that."

But Buzz's eyes had already lit up like beacons. "You're looking at the Conga Line King," he said, springing up and grabbing her hand. "Come on, baby, let's shake those maracas!"

"Oh God, *no*," Lauren groaned as he pulled her to

her feet, attached her hands to his hips and began conga-ing across the bar area toward the dance floor.

"One, two, three—*boom*!" Buzz chanted as the other conventioneers joined in behind Lauren and the band picked up the beat. The hooting and whooping was deafening.

"Buzz!" Lauren pleaded, but the conga king had abandoned himself to the bouncing beat, and Lauren had no choice but to bounce right along with him. Through her own moans of abject embarrassment, Lauren could hear Rene coaching her all the way from Seattle. *Have some fun. Live, Lauren, live!*

"Shake those maracas!" Buzz whooped again.

Oh, hell, why not, Lauren thought. "One, two three—*boom*," she chimed in, shaking her shoulders.

She was swinging and swaying with the best of them when a flash of golden hair caught her eye.

Him? Her mind asked the question even before her senses could register what they'd seen. Was it him? She craned around to see, but the line had swung in another direction, and she knew she wouldn't get another look until they came around again.

The room resounded with "One, two, three—*boom*!"

As the bar area came into sight, she saw him sitting at the end of the counter, half-turned and leaning against the wall. He was nursing a drink...and watching her.

She glanced at the ceiling with a muffled groan, won-dering if it was possible to die of mortification. Just let me *disappear*, she thought, invoking the Chinese curse again.

But she didn't disappear—and when she looked at

him again he was smiling. Just a little, the kind of almost-smile Lauren loved when rebels like Jimmy Dean did it in the old movies.

She smiled back, and felt foolish and silly and thrilled. Her heart was pinging about in her chest, and she wasn't quite sure where her feet were going anymore.

Mercifully, the music stopped then. As the dancers stomped, clapped and whistled, Lauren tugged on Buzz's jacket, yelling over the din, "Excuse me, will you? A friend of mine's here—"

Apparently Buzz didn't hear her. "Where're you going?" he said, grabbing her hand as she turned away. He twirled her back. "We didn't rumba yet."

"The lady rumbas with me, or she doesn't rumba at all," a man said over Lauren's shoulder.

Lauren spun around and stared up into ice blue eyes and sun-swept hair. Justin Dunne was apparently cutting in. He was still smiling, but by the way he was sizing up Buzz, Lauren had the distinct feeling that the conga king wasn't going to talk his way out of this one.

Buzz broke the stare-down first. "You know this guy?" he asked Lauren.

"She knows me," Dunne said.

"Yeah, but does she want to dance with you?" Buzz persisted.

"Ask her."

The music kicked in again, a provocative Latin beat. Lauren looked from one man to the other and realized she had a situation on her hands. Two men ready to fight for the right to dance with Lauren Cambridge? This was more progress than she'd bargained for. "Sorry, guys, I don't rumba."

"You don't conga too well, either," Buzz admitted.

Lauren shrugged and smiled apologetically into Justin's eyes. "I guess I'm one of those unfortunates with no rhythm."

"Well, hey," Buzz protested lightly, "you're not *that* bad. They probably have classes for, you know—the dancing-impaired." He scrutinized Justin again, then caught Lauren's hand and pulled her aside. "Listen, you gonna be okay with this guy?"

Lauren glanced over her shoulder at Justin's arresting features and rugged stature. I hope not, she thought. "Sure, Buzz. I'm a big girl. I can take care of myself."

"Okay, well listen," Buzz said protectively, "I'm going to find myself a dancin' partner, but I'll be around if he gives you any trouble, understand?" He shook her hand and backed away, waving. "You just holler, hear?"

"I'll do that," Lauren promised.

As Buzz disappeared into the dance-floor crowd, Lauren was aware of Justin at her elbow. "I don't rumba, either," he said under his breath.

Lauren turned to him with a delighted smile. Yes, she *was* delighted to see him again, utterly and unequivocally. She even felt a little breathless. Now she had some inkling why the annoying enraptured couples were so dewy-eyed.

"Who wants to dance anyway," he said, turning her around and pointing toward the open-air side of the dance floor, "when there's a sky full of stars out there. How about a walk?"

"Sure." As they started for the exit, Lauren had a moment of regret about the dancing. It was true that she didn't rumba, but she would have loved to have danced with him. Just the thought of being that close to him warmed her blood and threatened to set off the fireworks again.

They took a winding path through the estate grounds that led toward the castle. Lauren found the spotlit gardens beautiful, and the evening air balmy and fragrant and warm. Very warm. Caribbean nights had an undercurrent of moist tropical heat that was invariably pungent and steamy.

Lauren was aware of her cotton sundress clinging to her breasts and her legs, but the man walking beside her looked lithe and cool in a crisp white shirt, the sleeves rolled up above his elbows, and biscuit-colored slacks.

"Are you staying at the castle?" she asked as they approached it.

"No, I'm in one of the bungalows," he said. "I'd asked for a castle room, but there was some mix-up, apparently. Someone else got it."

I wonder if it was me? she thought.

"Maybe it was you," he said casually.

She glanced up and saw a smile flash in his eyes as they broke from the path and walked across the grass to the gardens behind the castle.

The fountains' spray caught the moonlight and sparkled like gems, stunningly iridescent. The flaming scarlet blossoms of the flamboyant trees were awash with lavender highlights, and the pink hibiscus petals shone ice-white.

Lauren felt her senses reeling a little at the mystical effect. There *is* some kind of magic at work here, she thought, especially at night. Turning to look at the castle, gracefully lit and eerily majestic in the darkness, she searched its lines and found the balcony to her own room.

"Have you seen *her* yet?" he asked, his voice hushed at her ear.

"Seen who?" Lauren turned, startled.

"The White Lady—Lucy." A smile caught his eyes again. In the transient light, the effect was whispery and enigmatic.

A breeze lifted Lauren's hair and made her shiver.

"She's the one who haunts the castle," he said, laughing. "Didn't you know?"

"Lucy? Sam Lord's Lucy?"

"That's what they say." He studied the castle, his profile intent. "There are islanders who swear they've seen her on the balconies."

"Really?" Lauren found herself scanning the castle again, actually thinking she might see something. A glint of moving light, a woman's form? She caught herself. He was kidding, of course, and probably highly amused at her suggestibility. "Sure, ghosts," she said, turning to him, expecting a smile.

The expectation lodged in her throat. He wasn't smiling. The breeze was rustling his hair and his hands were in his pockets, all very casual. But the interest in his eyes wasn't. He was looking at her as if she was someone he knew and couldn't place.

"Is something wrong?" she asked.

He shook his head, but even as he did it, something altered in his eyes. It was almost imperceptible, a scintilla of light, as though his focus had changed, as though he'd moved beyond vision to some image in his mind. The transformation was fleeting, an instant in time, but the effect was like a glimpse into a man's soul.

Lauren felt her heart beating faster. "Justin?"

He came back then, to the garden, to her.

Lauren touched his arm. "Is something wrong?"

"No…" he said, as though to himself, "no, it was nothing—a memory trace." He dismissed it all with a smile. "I guess you don't believe in ghosts."

"No, of course not. I mean most people don't, do they?" The fact was, Lauren had never given much thought to ghosts one way or the other. The subject hadn't come up all that often in the course of her life. But here, in this dark, ethereal place, ghosts seemed a topic that might actually warrant discussion.

"…this is the Caribbean," he was saying, "a world apart. These islands are a melting pot of arcane beliefs and superstitions. Myths and legends are a favorite pastime." He paused to glance at her, and his voice changed subtly. "Some of the islanders even believe that Lucy's ghost has certain powers over lovers who stay in the castle."

Now Lauren was intrigued. "Powers?"

"They say she puts a spell on lovers that makes them irresistible to each other. Everything they feel—desire, passion, need—is intensified."

"Oh…" Lauren met his eyes and experienced the most delicious and frightening sensation in her stomach. Like a sudden drop in altitude or a quick, breathtaking descent down a slide. Heat rose in her cheeks.

"Do you believe in ghosts?" she asked, more to bring herself out of the dive than from any burning desire to know.

"Ghosts, magic, spells—I believe in it all," he said, his voice low and faintly husky. "If you don't believe, it doesn't exist."

Lauren looked back at the castle and wished the night and the man and the moonlight weren't so persuasive. The idea of a haunted castle was wildly romantic—unless you had to sleep in one of the rooms.

Something brushed her leg then, a cool, furry thing. For an instant she thought she'd imagined it. Then she felt it again. *"Oh!"* she cried, bolting forward. She whirled in the darkness, and Justin whirled, too.

"What was that?" Lauren gasped.

A small animal's eyes flashed in the moonlight and disappeared.

Lauren screamed and grabbed for Justin. "Dear God, *what is it?*"

He laughed softly and pulled her into his arms. "It's one of the wild cats."

"Omigod," she breathed, burrowing her head into his shoulder, "like a panther?"

"No," he said, laughing, "like a house cat, only feral. The management tolerates them because they keep the rodent population down."

"Oh...a house cat?" She uncurled to look at him.

"Yup." He tightened his arm around her.

It suddenly hit her that she was in his arms, pressed up against his muscular body and staring into his eyes. Lauren felt that sliding sensation in her stomach again, only this time it was a sheer drop.

His lips parted, but he didn't say a word.

He didn't have to. They both knew what was going to happen. Stay with it, Lauren, she told herself, her heart thudding. But she couldn't. "Really?" she breathed. "A cat? Do you think we frightened it?" She turned her head, pretending to scan the grounds.

Justin let out a gust of laughter and released her. "Godzilla couldn't frighten that cat. I will give the critter one thing, though. Its timing was perfect. *Yours* on the other hand—" he cocked his head, looking more amused than exasperated "—is lousy."

"I know," she admitted, already beginning to regret her cowardice. He'd nearly kissed her. Now the mood was broken, and there was no telling when the opportunity would present itself again.

She was considering screaming and pretending she'd seen another cat when a rustling sound in the bushes made pretense unnecessary. Justin spun around just as a Bajan teenager burst through a thicket of oleander. He thrust a piece of paper in Justin's hand and fled.

Justin's eyes followed the boy and then returned to the note. He read it, glanced at Lauren and exhaled. "Sorry, I've got to go."

"What is it?" she asked, not meaning to pry. "Nothing serious, I hope?"

"No, not serious, but it can't wait." He stepped back, then nodded to her. "Will you be all right? I can walk you back."

Lauren waved him on. "Go ahead. I'll be fine."

She watched him stride away and had the strangest, sharpest premonition that she might not see him again. "Justin!" she called.

He turned back, and she began to walk toward him, not sure what was compelling her.

"What is it?" he asked, his hands out.

"Nothing, I just—"

Her heart was hammering so hard by the time she reached him that she felt disoriented. "I just wanted to say goodbye," she told him breathlessly, "that's all."

He looked baffled. "Yes, well…goodbye."

"No, not like that." An inclination came over her— an impulse she could hardly believe, and yet even as it occurred to her, she knew she was going to do it. Brushing her fingers along his jawline, she hooked his neck and pulled him forward. "Like this."

She kissed him. Rising on tiptoe, pressing her body to his, she kissed him with all the startled urgency of a woman awakened from years of denial. Her fingers trembled on his neck and her heart pulsed in her throat as she tangled her fingers in his hair, drawing him closer, deepening the kiss.

The rumble of surprised pleasure in his throat thrilled her. Suddenly, she felt his hands on her waist, climbing her rib cage, and a shudder of pleasure stroked through her. Breathlessly, she drew back, lightening the pressure, dragging her mouth over his and delighting in the soft prickle of his mustache.

A moan welled in Lauren's throat, and it came to her suddenly what she'd done, what she was *doing*. In that instant of reality, she felt as though some part of her had detached, that she was watching this crazy, breathless woman cling to this sexy, startled man. Confused, astonished, delighted, she wondered if she'd gone mad. Or maybe she was already under Lucy's spell? Whatever it was, she'd never felt so shocked at herself and so secretly pleased in her life.

Easing her fingers out of his hair, she broke the kiss and gently pushed him away. "My timing improving?"

"Definitely," he breathed.

She pointed to the message. "You better take care of that."

He stepped back, working the paper between his fingers. As he turned and sprinted away, she called after him, "My name! It's Lauren."

Three

Lauren sat on the canopied bed in her room, still smiling, her head still swirling with the sensations of the evening. She wore only a light cotton nightgown, her sundress in a heap on the floor where she'd left it.

"Vacations," she murmured, running her palm along the bed's silky apricot spread, "aren't half bad." Sighing out the excitement that bubbled in her throat, she fell backward with a soft plop and spread her arms like a child making angel wings in the snow.

"Look at me," she said, exhaling soft laughter. "Thirty-three going on sixteen. *God*, it's fun! I've got to call Rene and tell her what a wanton woman I've become."

She let the evening play back through her mind and felt the same delicious shivers of pleasure. Remembering Justin's surprised moan when she'd kissed him brought a pleased flush to her face. Only now, lying on her back, she imagined him as the aggressor, above her, bending to kiss her, and the anticipation she felt was exquisitely sharp.

Supine, with her arms flung out, she was acutely aware of her own vulnerability, and it was a thrilling and paralyzing sensation. Her limbs felt as though they were melting with warmth and a rapturous weakness. Closing her eyes, she could feel the heat of his mouth seeking her lips...his hands seeking her skin...his muscular legs easing her thighs open...

"Oh, God," she breathed, arching up to a sitting position, inhaling deeply, clasping her hands. The feelings were so intense that her palms were damp! And a fizzy sensation vibrated in her belly. Like uncorked champagne that wouldn't stop foaming.

She pressed her hands to her stomach and inhaled, but the feelings wouldn't subside. "I know this is all new and exciting," she informed her lower torso, "but I think we should take this passion stuff a little more slowly, don't you?" Her mind flashed an image of a nonswimmer, quaking on a diving board, on the brink of a swan dive. "Maybe we should try the shallow end and the water wings first," she suggested.

She stood and walked to the window, letting the fragrant breeze cool her face. As her emotional temperature dropped, the rational part of her brain began to revive, and with it came misgivings.

A romantic apprenticeship was probably a fine idea, she would give Rene that much, but was this the right place, the right time? She wasn't a beginner to sexual intimacy—she and Nigel had been lovers—but she was a beginner to passion. Never once in her two-year engagement had she felt anything remotely like her responses of the last twenty-four hours. It was remarkable headway, perhaps too remarkable. There was such a thing as too much, too soon. Beginners needed patience and gentleness, she reminded herself, and a safe environment. If tropical islands, ghosts and mysterious men weren't the advanced course, they ought to be!

Then there was Justin Dunne himself. It wasn't any one thing in particular about him that concerned her; it was the combination of incidents: the way he'd stopped the taxi, the uncut stone, his comment about her eyes, his odd silences...and tonight, the boy with the message.

Lauren's intuition was nagging her with warnings, as it had been from the first. She turned away from the window and moved to the wardrobe mirror, pensively studying her symmetrical features and gray eyes. She wasn't emotionally prepared for a man like Justin—not yet, not her first time out.

Maybe I shouldn't see him again, she thought. Maybe I should wait for someone safer, a gentle, patient man. The relief and disappointment that swept her in the wake of that thought was startling. She glanced again at her reflection, and the sparkle of awareness in her eyes alerted her to what she was doing. "Oh, *Lauren*," she said, "you nearly did it, didn't you? You nearly disqualified him. Just like you have every other man who reminds you that you're a living, breathing woman."

She shook her head, disgusted, and made a clucking sound. "Just for that, Chicken Nuggets, you are on orders to see him again. Tomorrow."

Pleased with herself, she prepared for bed.

Moments later, as she pulled down the bedspread, the apricot sheets looked so cool and inviting that she had a fleeting desire to feel them against her skin. A little stripping music, please, she thought, smiling as she hooked the strap of her nightgown with her finger and drew it off her shoulder. Hesitating, she was aware as never before of the floating feel of the smooth fabric against her skin. Sleeping naked seemed so decadent, so risky...

Oh, why not, she thought, absently aware that those three words were becoming her theme song. She released the other strap and let the material slide of its own weight down her body. Riveted by the cool, silken sensations, she stepped out of the gown and quickly slipped between the sheets, reaching up at the same time to turn off the light.

It was then, with her fingers on the light switch, that she hesitated, frozen in a web of awareness. For a second, something arrested her attention. Nothing tangible, nothing she could see or hear. She felt it more than sensed it, felt it on her skin and in her bones. Her mind had glimpsed something, a shimmer of light, a rustle of movement.

"Is someone here?" she whispered, pulling up the sheet and swinging around. She stared at the window, and the answer flashed into her mind. *Someone had been watching her.* Someone's eyes had been on her, she could feel it.

Gathering the sheet around her, she rushed to the window and closed and bolted it. The floodlit fountains illuminated the gardens below, but she saw no one down there, not even a couple out for a romantic stroll. Looking beyond the gardens into the placid, star-strewn night, Lauren remembered she was on the second floor. Anyone looking through this window would have had to scale the building! She couldn't imagine anyone wanting to see Lauren Cambridge naked that badly.

Closing her eyes, she took a huge breath and exhaled it. You really are overwrought, Lauren, she thought, hitching up the sheet she'd wrapped around her. Kissing men, sleeping naked, *imagining* Peeping Toms.

Her nightgown was still lying in a heap where she'd left it. She whisked it up, slipped it on, and then, feeling infinitely safer, she plumped the bed's pillows the way she always did at home and climbed back in. With the covers pulled up around her, she took a last look around the room. Satisfied, she switched off the light and rolled to her side, burrowing into the feather pillow.

What she'd failed to notice in her quick perusal was the green-eyed monkey silently observing her from its perch atop the wall mirror—its simian features looking uncannily real in the moonlight, and its faceted eyes glowing like stolen emeralds.

* * *

Lauren awoke to a wall of darkness, a scream on her lips. *Who's there?* her mind cried out, but her mouth wouldn't form the words. Springing up, she grabbed fistfuls of bedclothes and dragged them up around her for protection.

Who's there?

A silver ribbon of moonlight lit a path from the window to the opposite wall. Everywhere else the room was as opaque and unfathomable as deep space. Quaking, Lauren searched the looming darkness frantically. She knew someone was in the room. This time she'd heard the movements. They'd awakened her.

She found her voice, a reedy whisper. "I know someone's in here—"

A sudden rustle of movement to her left made her shriek and press back into the headboard. *"Who is it?"* she cried, twisting to where the sound had come from, straining to see the intruder.

Her eyes could discern nothing, but the rustling noises made her gasp again. "Who is it?" Unexpectedly, the sudden heat of anger spiked through her fear. "Who the *hell* is it?"

There was silence again…and then, a tiny, harsh cry. Lauren sat up, frozen with horror, the fine hairs prickling along her neck. She heard it again, closer, a baby's bleating cry, only raspy and sadder. It was coming from the floor near the bed.

She reached for the light and froze. *Something was on her bed!* She could feel its weight near her feet, and its dry, rattling wail ripped at her nerves. Lauren couldn't move, couldn't scream. Even her fingers were cramped with the paralyzing terror of what she might see when she turned the light on.

A sudden jolt of movement sent her screaming out of the bed. Stumbling, groping her way across the dark room, she searched desperately for the master switch on the wall near the door. She found the cover plate, the four switches, and flicked them all up. The room exploded with light.

Blinded, shielding her eyes, Lauren turned. She could hear her heart thundering in her ears, the skittering of clawed feet, the terrified bleating. Static danced in front of her eyes as her vision cleared, as everything gradually came back into focus, clear and sharp...her room, in living color. *And she was the only one in it.*

"What?" She walked to the empty bed, touching the bedclothes, lifting them. An angry hiss came from her right, spinning her around. "Oh, my God," she breathed as a cat emerged from underneath the antique dresser, its back arched, the hair standing straight up along its spine—a huge, unkempt calico cat!

Lauren sank to her knees, limp with relief, and let out a shuddering breath. "A *cat!*"

When she looked again, it had taken up residence in front of the dresser and was grooming itself as if it had every right to be there. It must be one of the feral cats, she thought, her dazed faculties regrouping. Perhaps even the one they'd seen in the garden.

"Do you have any idea how badly you scared me, you

furry monster?" she accused, her hands still trembling as the cat looked up at her. "Ten years off my life, minimum."

The cat blinked and resumed grooming.

"Lucky for your mangy hide I'm an animal lover," she muttered. "If I weren't, I'd take you home and feed you to Burger King, my eighteen-pound Siamese."

She managed to get to her feet, walk to the bedside phone and dial the registration desk. Glancing at the clock radio, she saw it was 3:00 a.m. The line rang repeatedly, and she was about to hang up when a man mumbled, "Desk," in her ear.

"There's a cat in my room," Lauren informed him, forgoing pleasantries, "a very large cat, and I'd like someone to come and remove it, please."

"Whatchewsay? Cat?"

"You got it," Lauren said, her sense of humor limping back, "and I don't want to be charged for double occupancy."

He grunted, mumbled something about someone being right there and hung up the phone.

That man hasn't a speck of whimsy in him, she thought, wondering absently if she'd packed a bathrobe.

Riffling through her suitcases for the robe, Lauren suddenly realized something. She hesitated, stopped, glanced from the room's locked door to its locked window and then down at the cat. "How did you get in here?"

Lauren was sure she'd just closed her eyes when the telephone began ringing the next morning. In her drowsy confusion, she picked up the receiver, mumbled, "Cambridge Investments, hold on please," and rolled over, taking the receiver with her.

The crash of the telephone to the floor behind her startled her to near-consciousness.

"Ms. Cambridge, are you all right?" a woman asked.

"Umm," Lauren murmured.

"Well, then," the woman cheerily resumed, "this is your wake-up call. We'll be serving a continental breakfast at nine and your taxi tour is scheduled for ten. Have a lovely day."

"Umm." Lauren rolled over, still clutching the phone to her ear, saw the morning sunlight flooding through the balcony window and remembered with a start where she was. The Caribbean. On vacation. Having fun.

The wild cat episode filtered back...oh, yes, someone had eventually come for the cat, one of the hotel night clerks with a net, which he hadn't had to use, thank goodness. The cat had gone peacefully. And then, she, Lauren, had passed out from sheer exhaustion.

Gradually, she became aware of the phone humming in her ear, raised herself up just enough to replace it and sank back into the pillows. Somehow, she had to mobilize herself for breakfast and a taxi tour, whatever that might be. And, of course, she'd promised herself that she would see Justin today. Should she call his room? She didn't want to scare the poor guy off. Maybe she would just leave a message, something subtle like: *More where that came from, Big Boy. Call Lauren.*

Breakfast went painlessly enough. Fresh juices

from local fruits, a croissant and strong, spiced coffee
were served in her room, continental style. Lauren
drank the coffee and got heartburn. It was going to be
one of those days.

A half hour later, dressed for the taxi tour in white
shorts, a halter top and a sun visor, she waited on the
castle steps for her driver. Apparently, she was to have
the taxi at her complete discretion for the entire
morning, with the freedom to choose whichever sights
she would like to see. Lauren vaguely remembered
telling her travel agent that she disliked the regimenta-
tion of planned tours, so this, apparently, was an alter-
native.

Her heart sank as she heard a sputter and clank and
saw the Rover coming around the bend. Tell me it's not
true, she thought, tell me it's not Duncan?

Smiling benignly up at her, Duncan pulled the
Rover alongside the steps. He looked almost seraphic
until his gold tooth caught the sunlight and blinked at
her like a beacon.

"*You're* the tour?" Lauren asked faintly.

He scrambled out and opened the back door for
her, nodding.

"I think there's been some mistake." She rose, one
foot already on the step behind her. "I'll just check
inside."

"Wait, wait! No mistake," Duncan blurted. "I take
you tour."

There was something in his voice that made Lauren
hesitate, a kind of pleading quality. Perhaps he would

get in trouble if she refused to ride with him. Caught between self-preservation and his sad puppy expression, she wondered if he was capable of safe driving—and then remembered that he'd settled down yesterday, eventually. "Do you promise to drive slowly?"

He nodded quickly, waved her into the car.

Against every reasonable instinct she possessed, Lauren started down the steps to his cab, wondering where the line was drawn between loosening up and risking your life. This time Duncan's smile didn't reassure her.

She would have been even less reassured had she known that she was being observed again as she walked down the steps and got into the taxi. Observed this time by human eyes, blue and very serious.

From the vantage point of his bungalow suite across the courtyard from the castle, Justin Dunne watched Lauren descend the steps slowly, his gaze narrowing as she slid into the taxi and swung her legs in last. Long legs, he thought, and then corrected himself, *endless* legs. On a shorter woman those sleek limbs would have looked like stilts, but she had the height to carry them. Probably could have been a dancer, he thought, smiling, if she had any rhythm.

He sobered as the taxi pulled away, aware that she'd had that effect on him from the first. She made him smile, even when he wasn't in the mood. She'd done it when she'd kissed him last night, and then called out her name…

That thought still in his mind, he walked from the

window to his bed and checked the equipment he'd laid out there: compact 10x field glasses, a compass, a small dowserlike metal probe, a bowie knife and the uncut stone to help him identify what he was looking for.

He picked up the knife, turned its glinting blade in the sunlight, then sheathed it in its leather case and tossed it on the bed. What would she have done, he wondered, if he'd told her he already knew her name...and a lot more than that about her.

He returned to the window, looked out and sighed. He should be moving, acting. Time was running out. The search was beating in his blood, and yet, here he stood, staking out a nineteenth-century castle, watching a woman get in a taxi and drive away.

He leaned against the glass, staring out, his forearm pressed to the pane above his head. The castle drew him like a magnet, as strong as the day he'd arrived. He couldn't shake the feeling that what he was after was hidden inside those sandstone walls. He knew that to search it now, with so little to go on, would be dangerous and futile, like the proverbial needle in a haystack. There was only one person on the island who could tell him what he needed to know, an ancient Bajan woman, and he had to find her. If she were still alive.

Several moments slipped by. His eyes were still on the castle, but his thoughts had reverted back to another woman, Lauren. Why did he have the feeling she was involved...or would be? Was it his intuition working overtime? Or his glands? God knew he found her attractive—and contradictory.

There was a cool surface to her, a self-possession that came with success, with knowing who she was. Most women never had it, but this one could have filed for the patent. She was sleek and slick, an 8x10 glossy, and that aspect of her challenged him. But then, out of the blue, she was someone else, a rumba queen, a breathless female who could tackle a man, kiss his brains out and then push him away. God, he thought, chuckling, shaking his head. Who was the real Lauren Cambridge?

He had a hunch she didn't know, either. She seemed tentative somehow, as if she were on the verge of some personal discovery and not sure she could handle what she would find. "Damn," he muttered, feeling his mouth pull tight in a smile again. Now was not the time for daydreaming about desirable women. If he didn't keep his wits about him, if he slipped up just once, he could wind up in a Barbados jail cell again—or worse.

He glanced back at the stone structure, his brow furrowing in thought. Bottom line, she had a room in the castle, and that could prove handy in the near future. What he had in mind was cold-blooded, but he didn't have the luxury of any other course of action. He had to use whatever came his way...and that was exactly what she'd done.

He turned back to the bed to gear up, but even as he pulled on the backpack, he couldn't shake the feeling that she was already involved, a key element in some way he didn't understand. Why? Those eyes? Damn, but her eyes had thrown him. That smoky color...like some kind of an omen. His gut tightened as he thought about what that might mean.

"Duncan, you fink, you *promised*," Lauren groaned as the Rover heeled around a forty-five-degree corner like a sailboat. The lush greenery and faded wooden shacks of the island's interior blurred past her eyes like an abstract painting.

"*Dunnncan!*" A full morning of the taxi driver's brand of hit-and-run sightseeing was all Lauren could handle. She'd been to the Mount Gay Distillery and the Andromeda Gardens. Now she was trying to decide whether to jump from the moving vehicle or thump him over the head and hijack his taxi. Suddenly he slowed up, wheeled off the road and shimmied to a stop.

Dust flew. Only this time there wasn't a man in front of the Rover when it cleared. This time it was a building.

Lauren dipped down to get a look at the ramshackle wooden structure through the front windshield. "Which is this?" she asked doubtfully, "the Flower Forest, the Wild Animal Preserve or Harrison Caves?"

Duncan craned around, smiling, and pointed to the legend above the building's door. Inexpertly burned into a warped plank of wood were the words: The Scarab.

Lauren surveyed the sprawling structure with

mounting trepidation. Plastered with posters advertising locally brewed beer, it had just the one door, no windows that she could see, and it was listing in the same general direction as the windblown banyans. Several rusting cars were parked out front, one with its door hanging open as though the driver had decided not to bother.

That way he won't have to open it again when he returns, Lauren thought with a shudder. "Duncan," she said, her voice lowered, "what are we doing here? This was not on my list of places to see."

"Dis place eat, drink," he said.

"Eat? This is a restaurant?"

Nodding, he shouldered open his door and came back to get hers.

Survival instincts took hold in Lauren. She shook her head, seized the door handle and held it fast as he tried to twist it. Rolling down the window an inch or so with her free hand, she said, "Duncan, I'm not the slightest bit hungry. Why don't we swing on over to the Flower Forest?"

"Eat first." He tugged on the handle.

Lauren held fast. "Flower Forest."

Duncan's jaw set stubbornly. "You come in," he insisted, wrestling with the handle and rapping on the window. "Important—see man inside."

"Man?" Without thinking, Lauren released the handle just as Duncan was putting some muscle into it. "What man?" she asked.

The door sprung free, swinging open and taking

Duncan with it in an eerily graceful arc, marred only by the man's frantic scrambling to catch his balance. As he disappeared from view around the front of the car, Lauren strained to see where he'd gone. "Duncan?" she called.

She climbed out of the car, peripherally aware of someone coming out of the restaurant at the same time. Duncan was sitting on the car's front bumper, disgruntled, brushing himself off.

"Are you all right?" she asked, adding as he grunted affirmatively, "You said something about seeing a man inside. What did you mean?"

Duncan raised his head, looked behind her.

Lauren turned to see the bearded, one-eyed taxi driver she'd narrowly avoided at the airport the day she arrived. He had a bottle of beer in his hand, and he was leering at her now in much the same way he had then. "You mean *him*?"

"No—not des man," Duncan insisted, rising, "hes boss, Jack Slater." He waved Lauren toward the restaurant. "You go inside, see Jack Slater."

Not on your life, she thought, edging back toward the open car door as the one-eyed man drained the beer. He tossed the bottle into the bushes and started toward her, an evil glint in his eye.

Lauren's mind reeled at the absurdity of this sudden threat, when, only moments before, she'd been playing tug-of-war with Duncan. She searched frantically for options. Duncan wasn't going to be much help, she could see that. And the Rover wouldn't be any protection against someone determined to break into it. She glanced around for natural weapons—rocks, sticks— but knew there wasn't time. He was too close. *A well-placed kick,* she thought, girding herself.

She heard the roar of a car's engine behind her and swung around as a blue, jeeplike vehicle the islanders called a moke wheeled into the parking lot and skidded to a stop, narrowly missing a parked car. Justin vaulted the moke's door, his gold hair flying, his eyes hard. He assessed the situation instantly and started toward Lauren, one hand gripping the bowie knife attached to his belt.

"Get behind the car," he told Lauren, waving her away. He moved in between her and the taxi driver, who'd come to a halt some four feet away.

Lauren quickly did as he said, and Duncan shrunk back, too, moving to the far side of the Rover's hood.

There was a split second of measuring scrutiny between the two men, and then Justin moved in as though he'd read the man's mind. Lauren's pulse jumped in her throat as the one-eyed man crouched down to get something from his shoe. "He's going for a weap—"

Before she had the words out, Justin had kicked the man's hand away, put a boot to his forehead and pushed him backward, sending him sprawling into the dirt. The hostilities were over in a flash of action, almost before they began. Lauren's assailant, apparently much drunker than she realized, was out cold.

Lauren closed her eyes, relief weakening her. When

she opened them, Justin Dunne filled her field of vision. He was staring at her, and there was a bona fide fury hidden in his blue eyes.

"Get in the moke," he told her, pointing to the vehicle.

His harshness startled her. And he was glaring at her as if she'd done something unpardonable.

"Get in!"

Lauren balked, her heart pounding. She'd had every intention of going with him—until he began to yell at her and order her around like some idiot child. "Why are you shouting at me?"

His jaw flexed, and she saw immediately that she was treading on dangerous ground. He was poised to act, and that could mean only one thing. She was either going to get in that jeep under her own power, or he would do it for her. And by the look of him, it wouldn't be a pleasant experience for anyone concerned.

"Move," he said, coming toward her, a dangerous glitter in his eyes. *"Now."*

She moved.

Moments later, they were barreling down a rutted dirt road, sending wakes of golden dust flying behind them. With the roar of the engine vibrating through her body and the wind blowing her hair, Lauren relived the incident in her mind while the man beside her drove on, shuttered and silent.

She was cautiously aware of the coiled tension in his body and of the fact that he may have saved her from injury, or worse. In the heat of the moment, his total command of the situation had riveted her, she couldn't deny that. But now, with a moment to reflect, she realized that his behavior spoke volumes about him, and very little of it was reassuring.

He was fearless, certainly, perhaps even reckless, and not remotely like any of the men she'd ever been involved with. From what she knew of him, he took risks almost casually, perhaps even sought them…and while that excited her, it also disturbed her.

She stole several looks at him in the course of the next few moments. With his blond hair flying and his facial muscles set in steel, he looked like some tawny golden animal. Beautiful, yes, but capable of savagery when provoked.

Lauren lurched forward, bracing her hand against the dash as he suddenly downshifted the jeep, and they roared down a steep hill. Her head was abruptly cleared of fantasies, but a million questions filled the void. Why was he so angry? What had she done? How had he happened to be at that place? And *who*, she thought, remembering Duncan's odd statements, was Jack Slater?

She had a hunch Justin knew, but from the look in his eyes, he obviously wasn't in the mood for an inquisition. Her questions could wait for now. She concentrated instead on where they were—and where they were going.

"Are we headed back to Sam Lord's?" she asked.

"Yes," he said brusquely.

As they zigzagged on narrow paved roads through

lush vegetation, Lauren experienced an increasing awe of the junglelike atmosphere of the island's uninhabited interior. Exotic birds sang in the trees, and monkeys scolded one another with whistles and barking sounds. It was a noisy, wild country, exhilarating and a little frightening.

The air was heavy with humidity and intoxicating fragrances. A person could get drunk just by breathing, Lauren thought with a smile. Even with the top down on the jeep and the wind blowing her hair, she felt warm and flushed, and a film of moisture dampened her breasts.

As they neared the coastline, she spotted a sugar factory and realized they must be on the western side of the island. She'd never noticed any industry near Sam Lord's. "Where are we?" she called over the engine noise.

"Bridgetown," he called back. "I thought we'd get something to eat before we head back."

She registered his voice, her senses so atuned to him she knew instantly that his anger had dissipated. He caught her looking at him, and for the split second that their eyes held, a dizzying current ran through her. She turned away, shaken. What was it that happened when their eyes connected? Why was it almost painful?

They came upon Bridgetown, the island's capital, from the north, and Lauren was impressed by two things—the city's natural coastal beauty and its crumbling disrepair. The streets were narrow and teeming, but not with cars, with humanity. Tourists—Lauren could spot them by their T-shirts—and locals buzzed back and forth across the throughways, oblivious to the blockage they created.

"The Cockspur Rum Sailing Regatta's on this week," Justin told her, navigating the crowded streets. They passed a courtyard prominently marked Trafalgar Square and walked onto a bridge that spanned the marina. He pulled the moke into a parking lot, vaulted out without opening the door, and came around to let her out.

"Come on," he said, smiling mysteriously as he took her hand to help her from the car. "I want to show you something you'll never forget."

Four

Lauren followed Justin down a walkway fronting the harbor. Rounding a corner, they came upon bright splashes of color and sound, a waterfront festival in full swing. Red, yellow and green banners flew from streetlights, storefronts and sailboat masts, and clusters of revelers thronged the area, laughing and dancing to the pulsating beat of a West Indian jazz band.

"Oh my," Lauren murmured, stopping where she stood. Her fingers slipped free of Justin's as she surveyed the vibrant scene.

Justin turned back to her smiling. "What'd I tell you," he said, reclaiming her hand and drawing her over to where he stood. "See the boats." He pointed to a line of racing sloops and motor sailers, thirty deep, tied up along the strip of waterfront moorage. "They're from all over the West Indies: Martinique, Port-au-Prince, Jamaica, St. Croix, Trinidad…"

Lauren was only half listening. She simply couldn't absorb everything she was seeing. A carnival of cultures swam before her eyes. A beautiful, dusky-skinned woman on the bow of a boat from Trinidad swayed to the reggae strains of a small, impromptu combo of Jamaicans on a neighboring boat. Seated on barrels on the dock, a French crew from Martinique hung together, mugs of beers raised as they sang along.

The sounds and sights were arresting, but it was the people who truly captured Lauren's imagination. Everywhere, suntanned, scantily clad bodies of all nationalities, male and female, ancient and youthful, pranced and danced and jostled for space. Concentrated as they were in this jutting rectangle of waterfront, they seemed to have risen from the sea, water spirits of every nationality.

"Come on," Justin said, interrupting Lauren's fantasy to draw her toward a restaurant aptly called The Waterfront Cafe. Its arched entryway was jammed with patrons and onlookers, but Justin eased his way through, Lauren in tow, and signalled one of the Bajan waitresses, calling her by name.

She smiled and waved them back.

With a minimum of fuss they were seated at a corner table toward the back of the restaurant, a darker and more intimate area, despite the crowds. All around them, the soft murmur of foreign accents—French, British, Portuguese and others less recognizable—were exotic background music to Lauren's thoughts.

Watching Justin as he ordered drinks, Lauren tried to recall their brief opening conversation in the taxi the day before. "Didn't you say you'd sailed in from Trinidad?" she asked him as the waitress left.

He nodded. "I've been vacationing in the islands for the past month." Glancing past her to the festivities outside, he added, "This is the place to be if you've got wind riding in your blood."

"So you have a boat? Here?"

"Yes, it's out front, *The Witch Doctor*. Maybe you'd like to see it when we finish eating."

"*The Witch Doctor*," Lauren murmured, struck by the name. "I'd love to see it."

The waitress appeared with powerful rum drinks and steaming bowls of callaloo, a pungent stew swimming with okra, spinach, crabmeat and seasonings. One whiff of it and Lauren's mouth began to water. In all the confusion, she hadn't realized how hungry she was.

After the soup, Justin coaxed her into trying everything from breaded flying fish to shrimp St. Jacques to a local staple of rice and pigeon peas cooked in coconut milk. The exotic spices, potent drinks and festive atmosphere were a heady combination for Lauren, the inexperienced vacationer. Justin was right, she thought, languorously taking a sip of her drink. I'm learning fast. She glanced at him and smiled, aware that he was pretty heady stuff, as well...for Lauren, the inexperienced romantic.

Suddenly it occurred to her that not two hours before

he'd been furious with her, and she still didn't know why. She set her drink down, ran two fingers around the rim of the glass, aware of warmth and a soft, fuzzy glow in her head. Finally, she looked up at him. "You were angry with me back there—at that place, I mean—The Scarab. Why?"

He looked a little startled, and then a glint of anger reappeared. "The Scarab is a dive, a den of thieves. Why the hell did you want to go there?"

"I didn't *want* to go there. That's where Duncan took me." Shanghaied was a better word, Lauren thought, remembering the name Duncan had mentioned. "Have you ever heard of a man named Jack Slater?"

Justin picked up his glass, took a drink, and then pressed the rim against his lower lip briefly. "Yeah, I've heard of him. He owns The Scarab. Why?"

"I don't know. Duncan mentioned his name. It wasn't clear in all the confusion, but I think Duncan wanted me to talk to him for some reason."

Justin bridled then, visibly.

Lauren felt her nerves jump as he sat forward in the chair.

"Let me suggest two things to you," he said bluntly. "First, find yourself a new cab driver. Duncan obviously isn't a man to be trusted. And second, don't, under any circumstances, go back to The Scarab. I don't know Jack Slater well, but I can tell you he's bad news."

"Why would a man like that want to talk to me?"

He took another drink, rubbed his thumb along the restaurant's logo emblazoned on the glass. "It probably had nothing to do with you personally——beyond the fact that you're an American tourist, and by this island's standards, wealthy. It wouldn't surprise me a bit if Slater arranged to have people brought to The Scarab so he can conveniently fleece them."

"Fleece them? How?"

He shrugged. "An illegal gambling operation, phony gems or artifacts, maybe even drugs. There are plenty of ways to scam an unsuspecting tourist."

Lauren was beginning to see that there was another side to this sunny tropical island, a distinctly darker side. She had a better understanding of Justin's anger now, but something about him gave her pause. His features were guarded, his eyes shuttered, as though there was more to it than he was telling her. She'd had that feeling about him all along——that his comments and remarks, no matter how casual, were just the tip of an iceberg.

A Caribbean iceberg? she thought ironically, staring at her own hands, nervously entwined.

His touch caught her off guard.

He brushed one of her wrists with his fingertips, then clasped it lightly and tugged her fingers apart, sparking nerves clear up her arm. Her head snapped up, and she saw the dark shadings of concern in his eyes.

Oh God, she was doing it again. He'd rescued her, and now he was warning her for her own good and she was making him out to be a man of suspicious character. She smiled into his eyes and felt her heart catch. Hitchhiker, you must frighten me a whole lot, she acknowledged silently.

"Ready for a sail?" he asked.

"*Yes.*"

It had never occurred to her to say no, she realized as they left the restaurant, or even to hesitate. Given her instinctive fears, her responsiveness to him was nothing short of incredible. She smiled inwardly. God, the spontaneity was so unlike her.

As they worked their way through crowds that were beginning to get unruly and aggressive, Justin drew her in front of him, cradling her protectively, guiding her along. Finally, as the congestion cleared, she saw what they'd been moving toward, a gleaming white and blue thirty-five-foot sloop secured at the end of the concrete pier.

"There she is," he said, "*The Witch Doctor.*"

"Beautiful," Lauren acknowledged, but she wasn't referring entirely to the boat. After an appreciative glance at the sloop, she'd tilted her head back and looked up at Justin, at the blunt line of his jaw, at the charge of energy in his eyes. Even peripherally, it was electrifying.

She waited for him to glance down, to catch her mesmerized, but he didn't seem to be aware of her scrutiny. Without a word, he took hold of her arms and drew her back against him, clasping his hands around her waist.

The sudden contact with his body was stunning. Lauren felt the muscular hardness and heat of him from the base of her spine to the width of her shoulders. She'd heard of lightning-bolt sensations, but she'd never had one until that moment. She wasn't even remotely prepared. There was no warning, no signal. It came all at once, a laser of light that flashed along muscles and nerves, galvanizing her for a second, arcing through her like a current, and then leaving her limp.

"God," she breathed, feeling the strength drain out of her. She relaxed into him, though not intentionally. It was a reflexive thing she had no control over.

"Hey," he said, laughing, catching her. One of his arms encased her, the other anchored her at the waist and secured her against him. Surprised by his strength, she closed her eyes and drifted, letting his body become her support system. It was enthralling to Lauren, the sensation of letting go. It was a dizzingly sweet initiation into surrender for a woman who'd never allowed herself to lean on anyone, never allowed herself to experience a man's strength.

He cradled her that way for several seconds, just held her silently without asking her what had happened. When she stirred, he bent and whispered, "I want to take you sailing. Come with me."

She heard the word *yes* shimmering in her mind, and even as she said it, she was wondering what was happening to her, why her reactions to this man were so intense...and whether she would ever be able to say no to him.

They sailed with the wind toward Martinique, cutting an arc through turquoise swells and lacy foam. The sun rolled in front of them, a ball of white fire in the sky, its rays flashing across the water. Off the sloop's stern, the island was disappearing in a hazy mist of pink coral beaches and palm trees bowing in the trade winds.

Lauren was stretched out on the bow, sunbathing.

Justin was at the wheel, his eyes on the sea, his mind on the woman. He was remembering her reaction on the dock, her weight against his body, the sudden surrender of her defenses. More than that, he was remembering his own response, the surge of energy to his muscles, the flash of desire in his groin.

Looking at her now, stretched out on the bow, he felt that twist of pleasure again, but this time he did nothing to suppress it. He was already anticipating what it would be like to make love to her, already imagining the subtle pressure of her long, sleek limbs around him. Lying in a haze of sunshine, she was more than beautiful, she was mystical, a sacrifice to the sun.

A swell caught the sloop, and Justin was subliminally aware of the chrome wheel's polished surface as it slid through his hands. His gut muscles tightened at the sensation. Easy, man, he thought, aware of the driving forces inside him. They were as strong as he'd ever felt before, and he was wary of the vulnerability that came with needing a woman. Especially now. But his intuition told him she was ready, too. He'd felt the languid heat of her body against his, the urgency in her heartbeat. She would be sweet and wild, and uninhibited—somehow he knew that, too, and yet something held him back.

A low sound, too cold to be laughter, emitted from

his throat. He had a beautiful woman captive on his boat, a soft, warm and willing woman…and he was reluctant to take advantage of the situation.

Why? His mind searched for an answer. His body provided one. The tightness in his gut was warning him to move slowly, that an involvement with her might be more than he'd bargained for. Starting with a woman like this would be easy; stopping would be hell.

The rustle of the mainsail pulled his attention. He'd lost the wind. He came about, taking a starboard course, and watched the sails fill up again, billowing, straining at the seams. The sight gave him pleasure, and oddly, a sense of mastery. The forces of nature always seemed to have that effect, inspiring and empowering him, challenging him to focus himself, to conquer them if he could.

Now the wind seemed to be reminding him why he was on the island. And what he still had to do.

Lauren stirred on the deck. Watching her draw up a leg and stretch languorously, he wondered what the hell was wrong with him. The stakes were high, his time was running short and he wanted her. He had everything to gain from taking her to bed, nothing to lose, and yet his dual purposes disturbed him. The kind of access to the castle—and her room—that a lover would have could work to his benefit eventually. He also suspected that was exactly what was playing hell with his conscience, the nagging belief that he would be using her.

He exhaled heavily, wondered what kind of a fool he was, and turned away to the sea, a power he understood.

Opening her eyes slowly, blinking away sunspots,

Lauren gazed up at the expanse of blue above her and felt a sigh in her throat. Through her warm languor, she felt a tug of wistfulness. This was indescribably beautiful, all of it, the boat, the water...and the man, she thought, turning her head to look at him.

She caught his profile, and the word that came to mind was strength—quiet, chiseled strength. God, how that quality attracted her. The inner quickening she felt brought her years of denial into sharp focus. Work had been her lover, her only outlet. It had consumed all her energies, leaving her too drained to want more. She had the trophies, the successes, but the rewards, she realized sadly, weren't worth the price. She'd missed so much of life and denied herself in so many ways. Passion and beauty, adventure...all the things that stirred the blood and the heart.

She rolled to her side and sat up slowly, stretching again, smiling suddenly as he turned to look at her. From this vantage point she could see that he'd removed his shirt, and the unexpected sight was enough to threaten her breathing. With sunlight streaming in his hair and washing the sunburned breadth of his shoulders, he looked too imposing to be real, a statue carved from the elements.

She'd forgotten she was smiling until he smiled back at her. His eyes were so blue and intent, so singularly focused on her that she felt a shivery little thrill, almost painful. And then she blushed. Oh God, I'm regressing again, she thought, burying her head in her knees. I've got butterflies and chills. I'm not even sixteen anymore. I'm *thirteen*.

She couldn't help herself. That was what being with him had done to her. He'd made her so painfully aware of herself and every minute sensation.

"Come here…"

She heard his husky voice through her crossed arms and took a deep breath. *No*, she thought, playing with the word, wondering if she would ever find the strength to say it to him, even if she needed to.

"*Lauren*…come here."

The way he said her name was spellbinding.

She went to him.

They stood together at the wheel, facing an endless horizon, the wind rustling their hair, the sun glinting off their browned bodies.

For Lauren, in that moment, cradled against his chest, sheltered by his arms, anything was possible. There were infinite opportunities for happiness. The adult part of her knew this was all a dream born of tropical islands and sunshine, but the child part of her was lost in its magic. The child part of her believed.

For Justin there was a kind of ache in his soul as he thought about loving this woman…and hurting her.

They sailed that way for some time, until Justin finally caught hold of himself and realized how far they'd gone. "We'd better turn around," he said. "It'll be dark before we get back."

Lauren laid her head back, resting it on his chest. "Do we have to?" She turned in his arms to face him, an irresistible smile on her face, a breathtaking sparkle in her eyes. "Don't you have an anchor or something?"

"Anchor?" He scrutinized her and a smile tugged at his lips. His eyes were electric. "Does that mean what I think it means?"

Lauren lowered her lashes, suddenly embarrassed, acutely aware that she was flirting and feeling damn silly about it. "I don't know," she murmured, looking up at him. "I just thought we might, you know...stop for a while."

He laughed, a rich, deep eruption of sound, and shook his head. "That's tricky in several hundred fathoms of water, not to mention currents strong enough to drag us to Africa, anchored or not."

"It was just an idea."

"A terrific idea under any other circumstances."

"Yeah..." A little slow on the uptake, she added, "Africa? That sounds intriguing."

"Barbados not intriguing enough for you?"

"Barbados is plenty intriguing." Was he fishing? she wondered, delighted. "And getting better all the time."

His eyes narrowed, harboring a smile. In the next seconds, he seemed to be detailing her features, finding things there that fascinated him.

Lauren suspended her breath through it all. She wanted to ask him why he was studying her, what he was seeing, but more than that she wanted very much to have him hold her, kiss her.

He shifted his weight a little, coaxing her between himself and the wheel, encircling her with his arms.

This is it, she thought, her heart accelerating. She waited for him to bend toward her. Instead, he brought the boat around, the boom swinging, the sails flapping wildly until they'd completed the turn and caught the wind again. He slipped on the wheel lock, and they glided through the water.

"Smooth sailing," Lauren said, winking at him.

His smile thrilled her. It was luminous.

"What is it?" she asked. "Why are you looking at me like that?"

"I was just thinking that you're the most contradictory woman I've ever met. You've got eyes like water sapphires, legs like a Barbie Doll, and probably if you chose to use it, enough savvy to run the Pentagon." He paused. "But you've also got a streak running in you. I think the Bajans call it moon madness."

"Is that good?"

He smiled, touching her face. "Yes, that's good."

His thumb traced the hollow beneath her cheekbone while his fingers played at her hairline, capturing dark, silky strands and then releasing them. His hands were gentle, but his eyes weren't. His eyes had the diamond-hard glint of sexual desire.

Lauren's breathing went shallow. She felt a flurry of peripheral sensations, the wheel pressing into her back, the boat moving under her feet, the sun beating down on her head. In the competition for her attention, none of those things had a chance. They could have been happening to someone else for all she cared. There was only one thing that made sense to her, one thing that was real. His eyes and their message. He wanted her.

"This is it, isn't it?" she heard herself whispering. "You're about to kiss me, and—"

He eased his thumb along her lower lip, hushing her, a gesture that might have soothed her if only his eyes hadn't had that searing hardness.

"I'm about to do a lot more to you than that," he said.

He tilted her head up, hesitated for a second, and then took her lips in a swift, thrilling kiss. His mouth was taut and fiercely sweet to Lauren's senses. His hand on her face was alternately caressing and controlling.

"I want to feel you against me," he said, his breath mingling with the words.

She moaned a little as he locked an arm around her waist and lifted her to him. Her feet left the deck for an instant and then she felt him everywhere along her body, the heat of his bare abdomen, the jutting hardness of his pelvic bones, the thrilling muscularity of his thighs.

He was more than a physical presence, he was an aura, enveloping her, bathing her in male potency. His lips warmed her temple and flitted like a butterfly along the arch of her eyebrows; his teeth nipped at the soft flesh of her throat and brought her sharp, tantalizing pleasure.

Reeling with the abruptness of it all, Lauren was stripped of her defenses. The scent of him was in her nostrils, the taste of him on her lips. He was urgency, heat and sinew. Now she understood what the brief glimpse of forces beyond her control had meant. The unalterable course she'd sensed was this aching sweetness that flared up in her belly every time he touched her; it was thundering hearts and searing mutual need. Desire was a force in itself, as natural and immutable as if she'd been gathered up and carried along on a surging tide.

His breath rustled in her hair, his mouth was warm at her ear. "Did you feel me watching you while you were lying out on the bow," he said. "I was jealous of the sun, of the way it caressed you and warmed your body."

She felt the pressure of his hand in the small of her back, his fingers sinking into the firm flesh of her hip. Seconds later, too soon for her to catch a breath, he was cupping her hipbone, urging her into the fit of his thighs.

His arousal startled her. She'd been aware of it before against her thigh, but now, pressed into the curve of her belly, its rigid heat felt uncompromising. She reached behind her to stay his hand, but he caught her wrist and held her that way, kissing her deeply.

Arched against him, she was drawn into a dark, erotic vortex where only the honeyed heat of his lips existed. Moaning in her throat, she caught her arms around his neck, and they spiraled together, like plumes of smoke caught in a down draft.

Just as she knew they would never come out of the spin, he broke the kiss, releasing her, drenching her with sensual murmurs and caresses. Some part of her tried to recover, but it was too late. She was in thrall, a moth to his flame.

"I wanted to touch you here...and here," he said, his voice a roughened caress as he feathered the bare skin of her midriff, his hand climbing toward her rib cage, "just like the sun." As he untied her halter top and cupped her breast, Lauren was reduced to melting softness and tiny inner cries of pleasure.

Justin felt her shudder under his hands and a flash of heat surged into his muscles. Her exposed breast was stirringly beautiful, full and firm, the color of cream with a dusky aureole. Aroused, he slipped the halter straps off her shoulders and let the garment fall to the deck, baring her to the waist. The sight of her almost left him breathless. The quivery sigh that came from her throat was like a fist closing around his heart.

She glanced down at herself as though she couldn't believe what was happening, then up at him, an expression of such naked alarm and bewilderment on her face that he felt himself hesitating. He'd been sure of her before, of her readiness. Now he wasn't sure of anything but the pressure in his groin. He was ready, yes—but he wouldn't take her, not unless she wanted it, too.

Fear sparkled in her eyes, glittery and beautiful as it lurked behind the dusky irises. "Lauren, are you okay?" he asked, feeling a shudder cross her skin.

She shook her head, emitting a sound that might have been laughter if it hadn't been so tight with panic.

Her reaction completely baffled him. He ran his hand down her arm, controlling the pressure, careful not to make it a sexual caress. "It's okay," he said, his voice taut. "We don't have to do this now, here." His stomach muscles were steel bands reminding him of the control it took to show this sudden sensitivity.

She inhaled, more a gasp than a breath, and her breasts shivered with the movement of her shoulders. A breeze blew across her body, tautening her nipples.

She's cold, he realized, and he gathered her into his arms to warm her, to shelter her. "Hey, take it easy," he said gently, acutely aware of her naked breasts and of every other inch of the lithe, beautiful body that was pressed to his.

She whispered a soft thank you, and sighed against his chest.

He bent back to look at her, already regretting his decision. "Thank you? What does that mean?"

She tried to smile up at him, but her lower lip was far too unsteady. "It means that you understand—and I appreciate it."

"What is it I understand?"

"That I couldn't go through with it. Oh God," she moaned, embarrassed, "I'm sorry, I panicked, I just froze. I had this feeling that something crazy was happening, that it was out of our control...or at least out of my control." She shook her head. "I don't know what's happening to me. I know this sounds strange, but I feel so light-headed, so woozy, like I've been drugged or something. I think it's the boat, the waves, the sunshine...and *you*."

Her smile was acutely self-conscious, even self-deprecating, but there was an urgency in her voice that told him she was serious.

"Hey, it's okay," he said. "Take it easy."

"Thank you," she repeated, touching his face. Then she kissed him lightly near his mouth, bobbing up and down on her toes to do it and driving him wild with the movements of her body. "There's something I have to do," she said, "and I have to do it now. Would you please take me back?"

"Sure." Curious, he added, "What is it?"

Eyes that were smoky and beautiful and still a little shell-shocked by passion stared up at him. "I have to call my psychiatrist."

Five

"I think I've been drugged, Rene!" Lauren strained to be heard through bursts of static fuzzing the phone line.

"Drugs? What do you mean?" Rene demanded, her voice suddenly clear as a bell. "And Lauren, please slow down and stop shouting. The connection is fine."

For the moment, Lauren thought grimly. The intermittent static was fraying her nerves. "Sorry, I'm a little anxious, that's all. It's this place, Rene, this island. It's getting to me."

"What's this about drugs?"

"I said drugged, Rene, *drugged*...by steam heat and spicy foods, exotic drinks and air that smells like someone bombed the perfume section at Nordstroms. I swear to you, Rene, this air is making me drunk."

Rene's soft laughter held soothing reminders of

home, where the weather was cool and the friendships were warm, and safe. "So be drunk," she said. "You're on vacation. Have some fun."

"I *am* having fun, Rene. I'm having so much fun it's terrifying. Do you realize the sun shines every day here? Is that healthy?"

"Ah, yes," Rene sighed, breaking in, "the workaholic on vacation. I recognize the symptoms: anxiety, incipient paranoia, and—let me guess—sleeplessness and guilt, too?"

"Rene," Lauren warned, "don't make fun."

"Sorry," Rene said, her voice gentling again, "but you are being something of a baby about this, Lauren."

"Hear me out, Doc. I happen to be in the midst of a personal crisis."

The line crackled with interference. "Give me the details," Rene called through the noise. "I'll walk you through it."

"He's about six-three, blond and gorgeous."

"A *man*?"

"Umm...and with enough animal magnetism for ten men. He's a heavy hitter, Rene. I don't know if I'm coming or going."

"Sounds like a bad case of infatuation."

Lauren smiled ruefully. "Is that terminal? Because I think I'm dying of it, a slow and agonizing death."

"That bad? Fill me in," Rene pressed, her tone warm and gossipy. "I want every detail, no matter how trivial."

"Is this my shrink talking?"

"Heck, no. This is the ten-year veteran of a stable,

but relatively unexciting, marriage who's going to live vicariously through the romantic exploits of her nervous friend. Get talkin'."

Lauren was feeling a bit disgruntled at Rene's lack of professionalism. "Sorry to disappoint you," she said, wondering if she should have called Dr. Ruth instead, "but there haven't been any exploits yet. At least not the particular exploit you're thinking about."

"Okay, then, let me put it another way, Cookie. Has he tried anything?"

"Well…yes."

"And—"

"And?"

"Details, Lauren, *details*. How far did things go?"

Lauren sighed. Rene obviously wasn't willing to play psychiatrist on this one. She wanted down-and-dirty, woman-to-woman, powder-room talk. "Second base. He tried to steal third."

"And—"

"And then he stopped. He got concerned. Told me we didn't have to do anything."

"Lauren! What are you worried about? This man sounds like a dream! A gorgeous dream, by your own definition, complete with a six-foot-three body and a sensitive nature. Marry him, for heaven's sake."

"Rene, will you please remember that you're a healer of troubled minds and nervous spirits, and I have both at the moment."

"You're right," she sighed, instantly contrite. "It's just that this is sounding too good to be true, Lauren.

What does the man do for a living? Is he geographically compatible? And the 64,000 question:

Is he married?"

"I don't know."

"If he's married?"

"Or anything else. I don't know anything about him except that he sailed in from Trinidad for some regatta."

"Well, no *wonder* you're nervous. You need information, Lauren, background data. Sit him down and ask him some questions."

Lauren supposed she was right, but the problem that really bothered her was more difficult to put into words. "Rene, he's…mysterious."

The line was quiet for a moment. "An interesting kind of mysterious? Or an organized-crime kind of mysterious?"

"If I had to choose, I guess…interesting."

"Oh, Lauren, this man is not to be believed. I can't tell you what to do, but if I were in your shoes, *he* would be in big trouble."

Lauren smiled, but she could feel the hollowness in her stomach and the phone cord was knotted around her fingers. She closed her eyes briefly. "Rene…I'm frightened."

"Oh…" Rene's voice softened. "Oh heck, of course you are. What's wrong with me? He sounds so much like one of my adolescent fantasies I jumped the track for a minute." She took a breath and was down to business. "Okay, Cookie, let's talk survival strategy. First of all, slow things down a bit. Clear your head and give yourself some breathing space. I know you're attracted to this man. I can feel the sparks clear up here in Seattle, and that's a real breakthrough, but there are other things to be considered. Is it more than a physical attraction? Do you like him?"

"I like him." Lauren felt her throat tighten with the resonance of those simple words. She *did* like him, perhaps too much.

"Okay then, hang in there," Rene counseled through rising interference on the line. "I'm going to leave you with some words of wisdom, Lauren. I didn't think of them first, but I wish I had: 'When you can't believe your eyes, listen to your heart.'" Static blitzed the line. "Did you hear that Lauren?" Rene called, *"Listen to your heart."*

Lost in thought, Lauren walked along the beach, pausing just long enough to sketch a heart on the damp sand with her bare toe and watch the surf foam up and wash it away. *Listen* to her heart? It was more a question of putting out an APB to *find* her heart! She'd had plenty of time to mull over Rene's advice through a restless night and the best part of the morning, and she was well aware that things had gone beyond the listening stage. Her heart had jumped ship and was with him, wherever he was.

She knew the next move was hers. He'd told her the evening before on the way home from their sailboat adventure that he would wait to hear from her. "Let me know if I pass muster with your psychiatrist," he said, his foot up on the dash of the moke, the half smile reflected in his eyes.

"My psychiatrist would adore you," Lauren had replied honestly. "She's a braver woman than I am in these things."

They'd said goodbye, shared a quick but dazzling kiss, and Lauren had gone straight up to her room to call Rene.

Now Lauren stopped and looked out to sea, lifting her head, letting the strong onshore winds whip her hair. This kind of indecision was anguish to a woman of her temperament. Her business modus operandi was analysis and action. Her strength was in decision-making. She'd always been a linear thinker, motivated by goals and tangible targets. Those qualities had served her well in the world of finance, but they didn't seem to count here.

None of that mattered on this damnable, mystical island, she thought. The rules were different. *Slow things down,* Rene had said, *ask some questions, get to know him.* Unfortunately, what Rene hadn't figured into that equation was the chemistry factor. Trying to slow things down with a man like Justin would be like trying to slow down a nuclear chain reaction.

A low wolf whistle jarred Lauren from her thoughts. She turned, and with some dismay saw Buzz, the conga king, heading down the beach toward her, a woven beach mat and a huge bottle of baby oil tucked under his arm.

"Soaking up some rays?" he called, doing an impromptu conga step.

"Flirting with sunstroke," she responded dryly.

Drawing closer, he gave her bathing suit the once over and made a pretense of honking a car horn. *"Ugga, ugga,"* he said, his voice cracking, "you could give a man a heart attack in that thing."

Lauren held up her hand. "Wait—don't tell me. Another imitation right?"

He grinned. "Pinch me, darlin', this must be a dream."

Lauren laughed softly and made a path around him, waving goodbye. She had no idea who he was doing this time, and she didn't want to encourage him. "Gotta go," she said. "Keep on dancin'."

"Speaking of which," he called after her, "there's a big bash tonight on the castle grounds. Be there or be square!"

"Wouldn't miss it," Lauren yelled back, without the faintest idea of what he was referring to.

She continued down the beach toward the castle, smiling, a little lighter of heart and step. At least Buzz's interruption had lifted her mood. It had also made her aware of her surroundings, of the wind in her hair, of the crowds on the beach. She glanced down at her suit, rather pleased at how little it bothered her to be strolling around in it now.

Never enthralled with her appearance, Lauren rather liked the dark, exotic look the sun had given her. Her chestnut hair, bleached with streaks of gold, lifted and flew in the breezes, and her face had a tawny glow with a natural flush along her cheekbones.

She also rather liked the glances she was getting from the male population on the beach. She'd rarely thought of herself in male/female terms. She was a working woman, feminine and appealing, perhaps, but never in the "female animal" sense of the word. Never the seductress or the sort of woman who knows the power she has over men and delights in it. Lauren knew the power of honed analytical skills well, but up until this vacation, she knew almost nothing about the power of her own sensuality.

Now, walking along the water's edge, she felt a little drunk with that knowledge. Buzz's reaction had been one thing, but the furtive glances and outright stares she was getting were another. Three days ago, she would have assumed it was because she was out of place. Now she knew it was something else entirely, something powerful taking shape inside her. She was giving off vibes! She was attracting male interest the way magnetic north attracts a compass needle!

She didn't have to wonder what had happened to her, she knew. The desire in Justin's eyes had taught her some new truths about herself. Not that she was feminine, not that she was a woman, she knew those things. He'd reminded her she was sensual, desirable, as much a "female animal" as any other woman on the planet.

The odd little dip in her stomach brought a wry smile. Ever since the sailboat incident yesterday, her body had been talking to her, reinforcing Justin's message with a barrage of signals: tight little twinges in the nether regions of her anatomy and a vibrancy in her breasts. Even the soles of her feet were ultrasensitive, reacting with tingles to the hot, white sand and cool, transparent water.

Lauren, she thought, kicking up mushroom clouds of sand with her toes, you are a fireworks display just waiting to go off!

When she got back to the castle a message was waiting for her. "Sorry, he didn't leave his name," the clerk said, handing her a folded note of just two lines:

There's a party in the garden tonight.
Meet me there.

Lauren halted in surprise, nearly causing a bag-laden bellhop to collide with another hotel guest in order to avoid running into her. Unaware of the confusion she'd precipitated, she read the note over and over again on the way to her room.

Meet me there. She didn't need a name. It had to be Justin. She was surprised he hadn't waited for her to contact him, but not at all displeased. The man was sensitive, but he wasn't a pushover. He knew she was apprehensive, and he was reassuring her of his interest. She smiled, aware that her reluctance about seeing him again had vanished like a rabbit in a magician's hat. A garden party? Delighted at the prospect, she nearly laughed out loud. And then she looked at the clock. Lord, so much to do, so little time!

She spent the afternoon combing the shops adjacent to the castle for the perfect garden party dress and found not one but two outfits with matching shoes. Afterward, she treated herself to a quick hairdo and facial at the resort's beauty salon and returned to her room. With just a half hour left before the predinner cocktail hour, she whizzed through the rest of her beauty routine with expert efficiency. By 6:00 p.m., she was dolled up, decked out and ready to go.

My goal-oriented nature has finally come in handy, she thought, smiling at herself in the armoire's full-length mirror. The new, white, off-the-shoulder dress with a swingy skirt went sensationally with her tan. Tucking her hair behind her ear, she let the other side fall provocatively over one eye. "A warning to all hitch-hikers," she said under her breath, "the female animal's loose tonight."

As dusk splashed the sky with a crimson tide, Lauren descended the marble steps into the garden. The castle grounds had been transformed into a Caribbean carnival with fire-eaters and contortionists to entertain the guests. Crowds gathered around buffet tables laden with food, and white-jacketed waiters darted through free-standing flaming torches, serving drinks.

Lauren scanned the festivities for a glimpse of Justin's white-gold hair. Twenty minutes later, standing by one of the buffet tables, a small plate of food in her hand, she was still searching for him. She checked her watch, feeling a little foolish all by herself and wondering if she'd misunderstood the note.

Disappointment welling, she picked at her food for another twenty minutes, and was considering leaving when she spotted Duncan hovering by a thicket of bougainvillea. Half hidden in its foliage, he waved her over. She started to wave back, then glanced behind her, thinking he must mean someone else. Me? she questioned silently, pointing to herself. What in the world could he want? she wondered, remembering Justin's warning to avoid the taxi driver.

"Hey, Rumba Queen! That you?" bellowed a familiar voice from behind her. She turned to see Buzz waving at her from the other end of the buffet tables, a barbecued chicken leg in his hand. "Lookin' swell!" he called out.

Good grief, she thought, first Duncan, and now Buzz, too? *Where was Justin?* She scanned the grounds hurriedly and saw not a trace of him. Oddly, Duncan had disappeared, too, and now Buzz was headed her way, two drinks in his hand. *Please don't let him do his Gerald Ford imitation,* she thought, smiling wanly as he shuffled up and offered her one of the drinks.

"No thanks, Buzz," she said politely, referring to the drink and to anything else he might have in mind. "I'm meeting someone."

His face fell. "Oh, yeah? The big fella?"

She nodded, holding out the faint hope that she'd discouraged him when a balding, rotund man in plaid Bermudas loomed up behind him and clapped him on the back. "Buzzbomb, you sonovagun, you been holding out on me? Who is this looker?"

Buzz punched the big man playfully on the shoulder, and they launched into a ritual of bumping hips, slapping palms and hooking little fingers. "She's a cutie, huh?" Buzz said, when at last it was over.

"Her name, gentlemen," Lauren broke in firmly, "is Lauren. Not looker, or cutie."

The effort was wasted. Buzz was busy signaling cronies and waving them over. "Harry, George, bring it on down! Yo, Cowboy, over here!"

Surrounded by beaming men with name badges stuck on their lapels, Lauren began to wonder if she'd entered the Twilight Zone. "You gentlemen are all Deeper Sleeper salesmen?" she heard herself asking.

"Sweeper," Buzz corrected, pride in his smile as he introduced them one by one, including sales statistics on each man. "And this is Squirt," he said, elbowing the large man next to him last. "He's our Power Steamer expert. Squirt holds the record for the most steamers sold during a Nebraska tornado. We're *proud* of this man."

His words packed such a wallop of emotion that a round of applause went up, and Squirt became the smiling recipient of a flurry of good-natured punching, elbowing and back-slapping. A chant began, "Squirt, Squirt, Squirt…" and suddenly, everywhere Lauren looked, grown men were bumping hips and hooking fingers.

"Guys, do you really think—" No match for the hubbub, Lauren simply watched the spectacle, disbelief in her soft laughter. What would any anthropologist worth her salt have to say about this? she wondered. Something profound, no doubt.

A curious crowd gathered around, seduced away from food and fire-eaters by the spectacle. Lauren tried to pretend she was merely one of the onlookers, as amused and amazed as everyone else, but as luck would have it, Buzz had something else in mind.

"Come on, men," he shouted over the din, "let's sing the little lady our fight song."

They stopped dead, exchanged glances and howled. Flinging their arms around one another's necks, they lined up like the Rockettes. Someone whipped out a pitch pipe, and to the rousing melody of "On, Wisconsin," they belted out, "Deeper Sweeper, Deeper Sweeper routs out dirt the best...Deeper Sweeper, Deeper Sweeper, swifter than the rest, rest, rest, rest—"

Their enthusiasm was infectious. As they ripped through the first chorus and into the second, the crowd caught the fever, whooping, clapping, singing along with them. By the third round Lauren was a reluctant convert. Laughing and clapping, she began to sing along with them, but deep in her heart, she was dreading what these guys might come up with next. Formation marching? A precision tumbling routine?

Wasn't it about time for Justin to show up and save the day? she thought, searching among the revelers for a sign of him. As Buzz's beaming face came into her line of sight, she had an awful flash of insight. *Maybe it wasn't Justin who left her that message?*

Halfway across the island, Justin entered the dark and musty confines of a cocktail lounge on the fringes of Bridgetown, surveyed the crowd and walked to the bar. Satisfied that the clientele were islanders rather than tourists, he ordered a beer. The bartender, a bearded Bajan, served him without comment.

Just as he had done at several other bars earlier that evening, Justin engaged the man in benign conversation for awhile, drawing him out and ultimately learning that he was a native islander, born in St. Joseph's, an interior parish.

When Justin thought he had the man's confidence, he said quietly, "If I were looking for someone who lived in the interior of the island, someone...difficult to find, who would I talk to?"

"Wot be this mon's name?" the bartender asked.

"It's a woman, a very old woman. I don't know her full name, but she goes by Soodeen."

Flicking the terry towel off his shoulder, the bartender began polishing the glassware. "You don't want to find her, mon."

"Why not?"

"She mixed up in bad things. Magic, voodoo."

"But she *is* alive? And she still lives somewhere in the interior?"

"I don't know, mon," he said, throwing down the towel and turning away to busy himself with other work. "I don't know nothing."

Justin knew that was the end of the conversation. It had gone that way all evening. Suspicious glances and frozen smiles when he mentioned the woman's name. Barbados was a small island, tight-knit and somewhat insular despite its relative affluence, and though the Bajans were often reticent with outsiders, especially tourists, Justin had managed to ingratiate himself with several of them—until he mentioned the woman. Then the walls went up.

He took a drink of the beer, dug some money out of his jeans pocket, dropped it on the counter and swung around, mulling his next move. The bartender's words had confirmed the rumors that the woman was involved in some form of witchcraft. When it came to black magic, it didn't seem to matter that the island had been colonized and Christianized by the British three hundred years before, the old fears and superstitions still ran deep. The mere mention of a voodoo priestess, as the old woman was reputed to be, struck even the hard-drinking regulars silent.

At least this man had acknowledged that the woman was still alive, Justin thought. That was more than anyone else had given him. Frustrated with his lack of headway, he pushed away from the bar and strode out into the humid night. The lights of Bridgetown flickered to the south of him and a salty breeze carried noises from the regatta. He'd scoured that area thoroughly, too. Nothing there but tourists, drunken sailors and savvy merchants more than willing to separate fools from their money.

He set off down the dark, narrow road, determined to walk and think for a while, to clear his head of smoke and booze. The interior of the island was Jack Slater's territory. Justin had tangled with him before and nearly ended up in a Barbados jail on trumped-up charges. The man was a snake, a dirty fighter who coiled in the grass and struck when you least expected. Justin's scalp tightened. One thing for sure, Slater wouldn't blindside him like that again. Not and live to talk about it.

A scuffling sound from behind drew his attention. He automatically gripped his knife handle, quieting his thoughts, slowing his gait. A quick glance over his shoulder told him the street was still, nothing moving but the shadows cast from a flickering streetlight and the steam rising from the rain gutters.

He continued walking, his senses alert to the slightest sound, his pace even and unhurried. If someone were shadowing him, he didn't want to put him on his guard. Within seconds he heard the noises again, and this time he was sure. He rounded a corner, slipped into the darkness of a covered porch and unsheathed the knife. Adrenaline surged through his veins, stimulating his senses, electrifying his muscles. No longer the prey, he waited with the deadly efficiency of the predator.

A form moved past him and hesitated, looking around in confusion. Justin flashed out of his hiding place, locked an arm around the man's neck and jerked him backward. "You were following me," he said, pressing the knife to the man's jugular. "Why?"

"No, please," a young man pleaded. "I'm on my way home, that's all."

Justin eased his hold and turned the boy around. He was a teenager, not much more than fifteen. "I've seen you before," Justin said, his voice intentionally harsh. "You brought me a note the other night at the castle."

The frightened young Bajan shook his head no, but Justin was sure this was the same boy. The note had been a cryptic message promising information that had turned out to be a false lead when Justin followed it up.

"Why were you following me?"

"I wasn't—let me go!"

Justin sheathed his knife but gripped the boy's arm to keep him from bolting. He was sure the kid knew something he wasn't telling him.

"I have to go home," the boy insisted.

"You're not going anywhere until I find out what you're up to."

A quick tug of war ensued with Justin, much the stronger, easily prevailing. "Either you tell me why you were following me," he said evenly, "or we're going to go to the local police and you can tell *them*. It's up to you."

The boy quieted, and Justin could see that he was deliberating.

"I'm looking for someone," Justin said, following a hunch, "a woman named Soodeen. Everyone on this island seems to be afraid of her. Maybe you know something about her? If you do—anything at all—I'll pay you for the information."

The boy's eyes glinted proudly, and he pulled free of Justin's grip. "*I'm* not afraid of her."

"You know where she is?"

The boy shrugged.

Justin took it as a yes. "Take me to her. I'll pay you well."

The boy shook his head. "If she sees you, she will disappear into the jungle like a wild animal. You will never find her."

"I have to talk to her," Justin said emphatically.

"Let me go," the boy said. "I'll find her. If she agrees

to see you, you pay me then, okay? One hundred American dollars."

Justin choked. "A hundred bucks? You sure you're not from the States? I'll give you fifty."

"Seventy-five?"

"Fifty."

The boy's face lit with a smile. "Fifty dollars," he said, darting away as though he didn't want to give Justin a chance to change his mind.

"Hey!" Justin called after him, "how long will it take?"

"Two, three days."

Justin watched the boy melt into the darkness and wondered how a fifteen-year-old kid figured into this tangled scenario. His mouth tightened with a smile. "I think I've hit pay dirt," he murmured, wheeling around, heading back to the jeep.

On the trip back to Sam Lord's, he had some hard thinking to do. About a woman, a long-legged woman with smoky eyes. He had a hunch about her, too. He strongly suspected she was going to be trouble one way or another. She'd already complicated his life with her hot-and-cold running sensuality. Ye gods, he thought, shaking his head as he remembered their encounter the day before. What kind of woman aroused a man to the point of mindlessness and then put him off until she could talk to her psychiatrist? A closet loony, he suspected.

In her defense, she couldn't have known what it would cost him to back off like that. He hadn't known it either, or he damn sure wouldn't have done it. He couldn't remember ever being that aroused before, at least not since he'd been a teenager.

He couldn't get her out of his head...the shimmer of her breasts against him when she moved, the startled desire in her eyes. He could still taste the silky heat of her mouth, could still feel her lush curves. He'd not only been excited, he'd been aroused to the point of pain with the need of her.

The moke hit a series of ruts, and he gunned the engine aggressively, gripping the wheel tighter, until the rugged little car finally hit smoother turf.

There were less painful ways to get access to that castle than through Lauren, he told himself, wheeling the moke onto the small two-lane highway that would take him to the other side of the island and Sam Lord's. He would break in through the dungeon entrance if he had to.

By the time he'd reached Sam Lord's it was nearing midnight, and he was exhausted. Still, as he pulled into the parking space next to his bungalow, he found himself automatically looking up at the second-floor balconies of the castle and wondering if she was up there in her room, asleep.

He felt the seductive pull of the castle, as though it were beckoning him. Two nights before, standing in the gardens with Lauren, he'd told her he believed in the hauntings, the spells, the legends, and maybe he did. Maybe he did. All he knew was that he'd never felt so irresistibly drawn by anything in his life. But was it the castle, he wondered, or was it the woman?

Six

Lauren stood ankle-deep in the unusually placid surf, moonlight flooding her like a spectral aura. Cool water lapped up and foamed over her feet, catching the hem of her white dress and tugging it along with the ebb tide. Her hands were in her pockets, her shoulders sloped forward slightly, and her eyes were on the dark horizon.

She could no longer tell where the sea ended and the sky began. The moon was so nearly full it eclipsed all but the brightest stars and blanketed the water like a sheet mirror. Ocean swells moved toward her rhythmically, the fringes of each wave glittering with white fire. It was beautiful, this night. It made her feel silent and sad.

She began to walk along the shoreline, holding her dress up, enjoying the pull of the water against her legs. It was late, she supposed, probably near midnight. She'd slipped out of the party on the castle grounds hours ago and gone to her room, thinking she might sleep, and then realized the futility with all the commotion below her window.

Buzz and his glee club had provided entertainment all evening, outdrawing even the sword dancers. The memory made Lauren smile. They were solid, those guys, solid as bedrock under the goofy grins and puffed male pride. She liked them. She might even have had fun if a certain hitchhiker had put in an appearance.

Apparently, the message she'd received hadn't come from Justin, a fact that left her more depressed than curious. She'd never had a chance to ask Buzz if he'd sent it, and unless she had a secret admirer, there was only one other possibility. She closed one eye skeptically. Duncan?

Continuing on down the beach, she let that mystery slip from her thoughts. At the moment she didn't much care who'd sent the note. She was contemplating her next move with Justin. Which, she'd decided, would be no move at all. This morning's spirit of adventure had fizzled out like a can of beer in the sun. Of course, he might still be waiting to hear from her—*Let me know if I pass muster with your psychiatrist,* he'd said. But she wasn't going to tell him her psychiatrist had capriciously advised that she marry him. She wasn't even going to call him.

"What's the point?" she thought aloud. "What could possibly come of this roller coaster ride he and I are on?" The way it was going, they would certainly end up in bed, maybe even in love. Then, in a week and a half, her vacation would be over, and she would never see him again. That was the way these holiday sprees went, wasn't it? Well, not for this cookie. No shipboard romances for Lauren Cambridge.

"Okay, so I'm a gutless wonder," she said under her breath, imagining Rene's response. "And wishy-washy to boot. Female animal? Make that a cowardly running dog." She hesitated, wanting to laugh, giving in to the impulse for a moment until her voice cracked and dropped to a whisper. "At least I'm backing out honestly this time. I'm not finding flaws. I'm not pretending it's his fault."

It's me that's flawed.

And frightened. If she could have chosen a man, *the* man, created him from dream stuff, brought him to life from the fabric of her fantasies, he would have been Justin. Strong and silent. Savage and golden.

Beautiful, mysterious Justin.

She kicked the water, sending a flurry of droplets into the air that became diamonds when the moonlight struck them. How could she miss a man she barely knew? Why did she feel this loss?

Stopping, letting the water swell around her ankles, she pulled up her skirt and wrung it out as though she could wring out her emotions with it. In the silence, she heard the lapping water, the swish of palm leaves overhead and the sound of soft footfall in the sand behind her. She dropped her skirt and turned. "Who is it?"

A form moved through the shadows of the palms and

into the moonlight. "I guess you couldn't sleep, either," he said, approaching her.

"Justin?"

His smile warmed and thrilled her. It wasn't a smile at all, really, just a tautness around his mouth, an energy around his eyes.

"What'd your psychiatrist think of me?" he asked.

"She advised me to marry you."

He lifted his eyebrow in amusement. "Interesting idea. Hasn't she ever heard of dating?"

He was wearing blue shorts and a tank top that shone silver in the light and emphasized his upper torso, a triangle of smooth, thick muscle over a broad-shouldered frame. Was it the athletic gear that made him look so powerful? The wash of moonlight?

"What brings you down here at this time of night?" he asked.

You, hitchhiker. "Just a walk…maybe to Africa," she said smiling.

"Walking to Africa?" He scratched his forehead and looked adorable doing it. "I think I may know a shortcut by way of the castle. They've got a great flamenco guitarist in the Main Brace."

Flamenco guitar sounded heavenly to Lauren. It also sounded dangerous. She knew where a couple of drinks and some sultry music would get them. Into trouble! "Could we go someplace quiet instead—and talk?"

"Sure…about what?"

"You. I need some background data."

He grinned. "I could give you a résumé."

A résumé? Instant data? She almost took him up on it. "No, I think we're going to have to do this the hard way. Asking questions, communicating, getting to know each other, and mostly…slowing things down."

"Why do I think this was your psychiatrist's idea?"

"I dunno." She shrugged. "It was."

His smile gave way to a low chuckle, and it was worth the wait. A flash of teeth, a crinkle of the golden mustache. "I thought she liked me," he said.

Lauren smiled. "She likes me better. We go back a long way. Besides, this vacation was her idea, and I think she's feeling responsible. Okay, let's start with your vital statistics. Age?"

"Thirty-seven, six-two, two-fifteen and eleven D."

"Eleven D?"

"My shoe size. Now you know more about me than my mother does." Casually, he dropped his hand onto the curved slope that joined her neck and shoulder. "It's warm tonight," he said, his thumb feathering her collarbone. "Let's go for a swim."

"Swim? In the water?" Lauren's heart started up. "I'd have to go get my suit."

"Why?" His eyes brushed her breasts, "there's no one around…and I've seen you."

She felt herself flushing. "*Please*…tell me about your mother."

"More background data?" He ran his fingers up the side of her throat and hesitated. His eyes returned to her breasts as though he was remembering something that had given him both pleasure and pain.

Lauren felt his fingers curl around the nape of her neck, and she was jolted with a fantasy of being pulled up against him, kissed deeply and roughly. A hot flush swept her skin. "Data," she prompted faintly.

"Oh, yeah…my mother." His voice had a faint husk to it, as though he wasn't as cool and silvery as he appeared in the moonlight. "Her family's from Dorchester, England. She's second-generation American, in good health with all her faculties, and she grows flowers. Tulips, she loves tulips."

"Really?" Lauren barely registered a word. She was distracted by the glint in his eyes. What she couldn't see was the source of that light, the energy gathering inside the man.

Even as he touched her, Justin knew it was happening again, the swelling in his loins, the tightness. The reaction wasn't unfamiliar, but his inability to control it sure as hell was. Cool water swirled around his feet. He wanted that coolness all over his body, relaxing him, soothing the heat. "Ever swim in the raw?" he asked, toying with the top button of her dress, buttoning it, unbuttoning it, watching her gasp.

"*No—*" her hand flew up to her neckline "*—*not even when I was a kid." She flicked her head, tossing back the dark hair that draped her eye. She was trying to look unaffected, he suspected, but he'd heard her breath catch, seen the sulfur spark in her eyes.

"Tell me about your profession," she said, fingering the neckline opening and keeping his hand at bay. "What do you do for a living?"

"I guess some people would call me a financial troubleshooter. I bail out ailing businesses, mostly heavy machinery…." Letting the words trail off, he eased her hand away, released the second button on her dress and felt the swell of her breasts beneath his fingers. The turbulence in her eyes was riveting. Her pupils were intense black dots suspended in smoky irises. She was excited, a little frightened, and that aroused him more.

"Justin, I don't want this to happen. I want things to slow down between us."

"I'll unbutton slowly…and then we'll swim slowly."

She half laughed, half groaned and pulled away from him. "*Talking* slowly was more what I had in mind," she said, backing up, her feet splashing through the surf as she escaped from him. One moment she was laughing, dancing to keep her balance, and the next she was in deeper water, floundering. "Justin!" she called breathlessly, and then her high scream pierced him.

He had her in seconds, lifting her from the water bodily, towing her toward shore until he could free her from the ocean's drag and pick her up in his arms.

Lauren writhed in pain. An agonizing fire seared the arch of her foot, as though she'd been assaulted by a thousand tiny, razor-sharp knives. "I stepped on something," she gasped.

He carried her across the beach, set her on an outcropping of rock and caught her by the shoulders as she swayed forward. "It's my right foot!" she moaned, slurring the words in her pain.

"Sit back and let me look," he said, propping her foot on his thigh, turning it in the moonlight to inspect it.

"Oh God, it *hurts*," she breathed as the agony intensified. One look at the tender, swelling flesh riddled with nasty little prongs and she was nauseous. A pincushionlike circle of thick needles was embedded in her sole.

"You're okay," he assured her. "You stepped on a sea urchin. Let's see how deep these spines are."

He touched one of the prongs, and as Lauren felt a nerve spasm clear up her leg, she arched in response to the pain. She swayed forward again. "I'm going to be sick," she gasped.

"No, you're not," he said firmly, hoisting her into his arms.

"Where're we going?" she asked.

"To pay a visit to the witch doctor. It takes a little island magic to extract sea urchin spines. In the wrong hands you could wind up with a nasty infection."

"Witch doctor? Whose hands are we talking about?"

"Mine." He trudged through the sand and took a shortcut through the trees. They reached the resort complex within minutes. Luckily, it was late enough that most of the guests were safely tucked in their beds, and Lauren didn't have to endure turned heads and curious eyes as Justin wound through the motel bungalows and swimming pool areas, carrying her as though she weighed no more than one of the slightly-built Bajan children who played on the beach.

The stinging had eased a little as they approached the

castle. This should liven things up for the night clerk, she thought, wondering briefly if they had a policy about witch doctors on the premises, or about men carrying women to their rooms. Her concern vanished as Justin strode right past the looming structure.

"Where are we going?" she asked.

"My bungalow."

His bungalow. She might have made an issue of that if she hadn't been in pain—and curious.

"That's where I keep the candles and the herbal potions," he said.

"How about some antiseptic and a pair of tweezers?" she suggested, grimacing. "Or better yet, general anesthesia and a foot surgeon."

"What have I got here, a woman of little faith?" He reached his bungalow and set her down gently on her good foot while he opened the door.

Little faith? He's closer than he knows, Lauren thought as he swung the door open and switched the lights on.

She hopped across the threshold, wobbled, winced and was swung up into his arms.

"If you lose your balance and step on those spines, you'll know what real pain is," he said, carrying her through a combination living room and kitchen area and into the bedroom.

He set her on the bed and bunched the pillows behind her, fashioning a backrest. Then, pulling a short black kimono robe and a dry shirt from the armoire next to the bed, he handed the robe to her. "Let's get you out of that wet dress."

"*I'll* get me out of it," she said firmly.

As he disappeared into the bathroom, Lauren fumbled open the buttons of her sodden dress, pulling it and the white teddy she wore off at the same time. Ignoring her throbbing foot, she stretched and draped the clothes over the lamp on the bamboo nightstand, hoping they might dry.

With the kimono safely on and tied around her, she had a moment to study his room. If it hadn't been for the Sam Lord's brochure on the dresser, she would have thought the bungalow unoccupied. There were simply no signs of human life, nothing out of place, no clothes strewn around except her own, no room service trays or half-filled glasses. It was immaculate. That frightened her a little, and she wasn't sure why.

"How's the foot?" He was standing in the doorway.

"Fine. Well, not *fine*," she said, aware that she'd been caught with her eyeballs hanging out. "Actually, it hurts like hell."

He walked to the closet, opened it and took out an elaborate backpack made of military camouflage material. From it, he removed what looked like candles, a small lime, some matches and a hunter's belt with snaps, hooks, several small pockets attached, and a wicked-looking knife sheathed in a leather case.

"What's that for?" she asked, her eyes on the knife.

He picked up one of the candles and rolled it in his fingers. "This is a witch doctor's secret weapon."

"I meant that other thing—the knife."

His eyes flashed to hers and held for a second. "I do some hunting," he said without further explanation.

She watched uneasily as he slid the knife from its case. The stainless blade, serrated across the top and grooved down to a razor-sharp cutting edge, reflected light like a mirror. Lauren had a distinct aversion to knives or to anything sharp. "Are you going to use that?" she asked.

"I guess I could bite this lime in half," he said, grinning faintly as he sliced the fruit into two neat sections, "but it'll be much easier this way."

She flinched as he sat on the bed, took her foot and settled it on his thigh. "Grit your teeth," he warned. "This is going to sting a little." He squeezed the lime, letting the juice run down her sole, trickling it over the embedded spines and inflamed flesh.

Lauren drew a quick breath through her teeth and bucked back as the juice hit the open wounds. "You *bastard*," she gasped without even thinking. "Let go of me!" She tried to jerk away, a cry tearing from her throat as the fiery pain exploded.

"Hold it," he said, clamping her ankle to his body. He twisted and gripped her arm, subduing her, staring at the shock in her features, the tears that welled in her eyes. "I know it hurts, but that's the worst of it. Easy," he soothed, his voice gruff. "The pain'll let up soon."

Lauren released a shuddering breath and fell back against the pillows. "Sting a *little*?"

"Sorry, couldn't be helped." He eased himself out from under her and knelt to get the candle and matches.

Wielding the knife again, he cut a chunk of wax off the end of the candle, lit the wick and began melting the wax down in a glass tumbler he'd brought from the bathroom. "I guess your pain threshold's pretty low."

Lauren glared at his profile. "What are you saying? That I'm a cream puff?"

A moment later he was coating the bottom of her foot with warm wax, dobbing it gently and thickly over the spines. Lauren felt its heat penetrating the tender areas and a drawing sensation begin. She sprang up apprehensively.

He pushed her back down, gently but firmly. "Sit still. The heat of the wax is drawing the spines out. It won't hurt, Cream Puff," he promised, winking at her. "This is the good part."

"How come I didn't get a shot of whiskey," she grumbled, "or a bullet to bite on?"

He was gathering up his gear and repacking it. "One whiskey sour coming up," he said, holding up the lime.

They drank whiskey sours and talked for the next hour, and Lauren was surprised and reassured at how forthcoming he was. He volunteered information about his business, mentioning that he was based on the West Coast and describing his work as a form of venture capitalism. Then he talked at length about his hobby, treasure hunting, which she sensed was his real love.

All the while they chatted, the wax slowly peeled off the sole of her foot, drawing out the spines with it. Lauren actually found the sensations rather pleasant and wondered if it could have anything to do with the whiskey sours.

A short time later Justin presented her with the sole of her foot after he'd cleaned it, and Lauren was impressed. The flesh wounds were still slightly swollen, but the redness and pain were gone. "Tomorrow you'll be as good as new," he promised. "No inflammation, no infection."

"You're really quite wonderful, you know that?" she said, settling back into the pillows and feeling gloriously warm and sleepy. "Is there much call for witch doctoring these days?"

"You're my first sea urchin victim this year. Demon exorcism is always big, though."

"Umm," she said, rolling to her side, "I'll bet you're good at that."

Those were the last words she murmured for several hours. Warmed by Justin's presence in the chair next to her, exhausted both physically and emotionally from the day's events, Lauren spiraled into a deep sleep, drifting through dreams of glistening seas, swooping gulls and sailboats, waking only once to see that Justin was still there, a glass of whiskey in his hand, a heaviness in the slope of his shoulders.

"Justin, don't be sad" was all she could think to say before she slipped back into the depths.

Justin smiled at her remark and wondered what truth it might hold. Was he sad? He'd been drinking slowly but steadily all night, anesthetizing himself, but never quite enough to put him out. He'd eased the tightness in his throat, dulled the unrelenting energy in his loins, but he couldn't escape the tenacious grip of consciousness. Sad? He didn't know about that, but he sure was in some kind of hell.

The half-naked woman on the bed was sweet torment for a man in his state of mind and body. The kimono he'd lent her had hitched up when she rolled over, revealing one long leg slung over the other in a graceful curve from hip to ankle. He'd considered pulling the robe down, but the thought of his hands anywhere near her bare skin was a test of will he preferred to avoid.

He took a swallow from his glass and wondered what she'd done to him. *Slow things down,* she'd said. What did she know about slowing things down when she was sprawled out there on the bed, innocently, agonizingly seductive. All his life he'd acted on instinct and impulse, taking what he'd wanted while the taking was good. All his life that strategy had worked for him— with women, with commerce, with adventure. What he wanted he went after. What he wanted he got. Watching a woman sleep wasn't his style. Not when he knew that woman wanted him, too.

He sat forward in the chair, compelled by the way her dark hair draped her face, the way her lips parted when she breathed. He'd felt the heat, the languor in her when he'd unbuttoned her dress on the beach. He knew the signs and sounds of arousal, and she'd had them all. The shallow breathing, the little gasp of pleasure. If she hadn't stopped him, if she'd let him strip the dress off her, he would have found her as ready as he was.

Almost as though she sensed his urgency, she

moaned softly and flung an arm out, grazing his thigh.
Her hand settled on his knee, and a shock wave of
desire hit him. *"God,"* he breathed. He wanted to roll
her over on her back and spread those endless legs. He
wanted to bury himself in that searing warmth of hers,
to lose himself in her outrageously beautiful body. And
then he wanted to sleep with her all night, inside her,
entwined with her, one body, one breath, one aching
heart. He swept up the glass of whiskey and took a long
hard drink, but the drive inside him built, twisting and
flashing like knives.

"You're not drunk enough," he snarled, rising and
walking to the living room, "not nearly drunk enough."

He strode to the window, staring out at the night,
breathing like a runner. There was a storm gathering
inside him, physical and frenetic, a carnal energy that
was eating him up. He knew its force and the brute
strength it took to hold it in check. Had it been any other
woman, he would have taken her to bed and gotten her
out of his system. But *this woman*, she got to him on
some basic level, triggering primitive male instincts,
possession and protection, urges he had damn little
control of. He knew that making love to her would only
whet his appetite, that the explosive joy of it would be
an irresistible rush, as hard to kick as an addictive drug.

He stared out at the castle, conflict churning in his
gut. Some moments later, he realized it wasn't just the
sex that was hammering at him, it was something much
more complicated and potentially dangerous. He was
caught between the mission and the woman. Did

winning one mean sacrificing the other? There was no question in his mind which was most important. The mission. It had to be.

He woke up on the couch, headachy, hung over, feeling like someone had drop-kicked him across a football field. Through his discomfort, he was vaguely aware of a blanket over him and a delicious odor wafting past his nose. Coffee? He took a deep breath, inhaling it. Maybe life was worth living after all.

He was struggling to sit up as she came around the couch, a steaming cup in her hand. "You're up," she said, making the obvious sound like one the prophecies of the Dalai Lama come true. Wearing the white dress and with her hair swinging free, she looked unsinkably bright and cheerful, a lot more damn cheerful than she had a right to be, *considering*, he thought grudgingly.

She set the coffee on the table, studied him reverently. "Do you know how incredible you are?" she said softly, sitting down beside him, brushing back his hair. "We spent a night together, alone, just the two of us, in this bungalow, and you didn't touch me. You slept out here on the couch. Do you know what that tells me about you?" The emotion in her voice made his chest tighten.

He didn't know. *He didn't want to know.* "What?"

"That you're one in a million, a sensitive and compassionate man, that you understand the importance of slowing things down, of getting to know each other."

Justin closed his eyes in pain and disbelief. *She*

thinks I'm a saint, and all I want to do is rip that dress off her body and drag her down on the living room floor.

"Are you okay?" she asked, soothing his brow. "Here," she pressed the mug into his hands, "have some coffee."

He took a drink and let its heat and richness flow down his throat. She was watching him raptly, concern in her eyes. God help me, he thought, she's enough to make a grown man cry. How do I tell her that she's driving me nuts! He swallowed the words with the coffee, sensing that it was as foreign for her to heap worshipful attention on a man as it was for him to receive it. She had the quality of a child with her first doll. She was too damn adorable to hurt.

"I know exactly what we're going to do today," she said exuberantly. "We'll get to know each other and explore the island at the same time. I'm dying to see the Flower Forest and Harrison Caves and the Wildlife Preserve, all the places Duncan was supposed to take me on the taxi tour. But this is better, isn't it? You and I can go together. What's wrong? You're not feeling well enough?"

"I'm feeling fine."

"You've already been to the Flower Forest and the caves?"

"I've never been to either."

Relief wreathed her face. "Oh good! I'll call the concierge for directions while you get ready."

She rose and started toward the bedroom.

Springing up, he caught her arm and whipped her back around. "I don't give a damn about flower forests and caves, Lauren. Is that clear?" He stared into her startled eyes and felt his heart beating. "We're going to make love."

A flush climbed her throat and burned her cheeks. "Oh, of course we are, Justin," she said breathlessly. "Just as soon as we get to know each other a little better."

The Flower Forest was everything Lauren had hoped for. Justin didn't seem quite as thrilled with the breadfruit and banana trees as she was, but that didn't dampen her enthusiasm. Lots of men found plant life uninspiring. He'll like the caves better, she thought.

They spent the full day sightseeing, and by the time they returned to Sam Lord's, Justin's dark mood had lifted. He'd actually laughed at the Wildlife Preserve. A gallows laugh, Lauren admitted, remembering his evil chuckle as he dangled her over the moat and threatened to feed her to the alligators.

Now, standing in his living room, perusing the resort's *Daily Activities Guide*, Lauren spotted something she knew he was going to love. "There's a shipwreck party tonight on the beach," she said. "They're having barbecued squid and limbo dancers. I don't think we want to miss that, do you?"

She turned to Justin on the couch, his feet up on the coffee table, his arms spread along the back. He was watching her with a single-mindedness that nearly made her drop the activities guide. She resisted the impulse to back away from him, from the odd, blue flame in his eyes.

"Unbutton your dress for me," he said. "Unbutton it slowly, then take it off...."

Lauren's nerves jumped painfully, and the activities guide floated to the floor. "We'll miss the party," she said, her voice evaporating as he stood.

"To hell with the party." He walked to her and stopped, not touching her with his hands, just his eyes. Incendiary, they flashed up and down her body, burning her breasts, her belly, her legs. Lauren felt their hellish heat all the way to her bones.

By the time he touched her, she was trembling, shaking clear through to her spine. "Justin," she breathed, her voice barely audible, "you're scaring me."

"Good, then that makes two of us." He snared the sleeve of her dress and dragged her into his arms, a crushing embrace, tangling his hands in her hair, pressing his lips to her temple.

Lauren's heart thundered in her chest. She was mesmerized and terrified as he rained kisses over her face and forced her head up with his hands. His lips smothered the cry of fear and desire rising inside her.

Justin heard the frightened moan in her throat, but it barely registered. His mind, his body were inflamed with need. It was only as he felt her go rigid in his arms that he fully realized what he was doing. He was taking what he wanted. He was satisfying his own insane drives and to hell with consequences.

Swearing under his breath, he ripped her away from him and held her trembling body at arm's length. *Not now,* the part of his brain that was still rational warned. *This isn't the time or the place to make love to her.* "I think you'd better get out of here," he said, his breath shaking loose the words.

"Get out of here?" she asked.

"Yes, go."

"Why? Where?"

He stared at her ashen face, her unsteady mouth, and he closed his eyes to summon control. Finally, exhaling heavily, he released her and walked to the far side of the room.

"Justin?"

He turned away from her then, raking his hands through his hair. He hated himself for the secrets he had to keep, hated himself for taking advantage of the situation—and of her. If he cared about her at all, he would tell her to get the hell away from him—and stay away. But he couldn't. He'd thought it would be easy, this plan of his. He was wrong.

"Go get your suit on," he said, his voice low, tight. "We're going to the shipwreck party."

Seven

Bonfires roared and crackled up and down the beach, spitting fire and smoke at an indigo sky. In the banyan grove the party was winding down, only a few clusters of guests left to clap and encourage the nimble male dancers who writhed beneath limbo sticks.

Huddled on an isolated stretch of beach, several bonfires down from the revelry, Lauren speculated on the mood of the man sitting next to her, staring into the fire. He'd been distant all evening. She knew he was increasingly uncomfortable with their platonic situation, such as it was, but there was something more than that bothering him. She was sure of it. There was something deeper in him that the silences covered.

She didn't bother to glance away as he looked at her, reflections of the fire dancing in his eyes. He didn't comment on her scrutiny, or ask her why she'd been studying him so seriously. "You cold?" was all he said, drawing her into his arms.

"No." Pleased that he'd come out of his mood, she snuggled into him, glorying in his warmth, in the sheltering strength of his arms. "No, I'm not cold."

He kissed her temple lightly and with such lingering tenderness that a question invaded her consciousness without warning. What kind of lover would he be? The impressions she had of him were so contradictory. There was a gentleness in him. She could feel it even now. But there was also the man she'd seen at The Scarab, a jungle fighter who dispatched assailants quickly and ruthlessly. What kind of lover would that man be? He was silent and omnipresent. He moved with a savage grace that she knew would come into play when he made love to a woman. Her mind flashed a split-second image of lovers tangled in a passionate embrace and the twist of excitement she felt nearly took her breath away.

"What is it?" he said, drawing her tighter, "are you sure you're not cold?"

She shook her head and shivered again.

"Then what is it?"

Turning in his arms, she asked, "Justin, how do you feel about making love?"

His eyes twinkled. "Is this a trick question?"

"No, I mean philosophically speaking. Do you think of sex as an expression of love? Or is it a more casual thing, maybe even competitive like, you know… scoring?"

He reflected on the question and shrugged. "I guess there was a time when it felt like a game, a contest to be won."

"And now?"

"Now? Now I think it's best when two people care."

She smiled, relieved. "Yes, me too. And I've always thought it was better to wait until you were in love...."

"Or close," he suggested.

She looked up at him and knew exactly what that meant. Again there was a kind of subliminal communication between them, hovering somewhere between the mind and the senses. She was caught up in the rugged beauty of his bone structure, the sensual wonder of his mouth. His was a mouth made to kiss, she thought, her stomach clenching as he bent slowly toward her, his breath rushing over her lips. She closed her eyes, waiting for the touch of his lips on hers and instead she felt a sweet little nip along the line of her throat, a flicker of his tongue in the lobe of her ear. The kiss, when he got around to it, was slow and sensual and almost painfully arousing. As he finished it, he brushed his fingers across her lips, sending an erotic tremor through her.

"Close is good," she heard herself saying.

He ran his hands into her hair and kissed her again until they were both breathless. "Even when I try I can't keep my hands off you," he murmured near her ear, a groan in his voice. "Come on up here," he said, patting his thighs, "on my lap, *quick*."

Every instinct Lauren possessed told her that was

going to be much *too* close, but the sensations inside her were overriding her fears. Slowing things down seemed irrelevant now. The only thing that counted was the man and this sharp, shimmering moment.

"Lauren, come on, damn it," he urged softly.

With the guidance of his hands, she found herself not only on his lap but straddling him, her legs tucked around his waist. It was a wildly sensual position that sent streamers of excitement running up her limbs.

She could feel every muscle in his thighs, *could feel them flexing* as he bent forward and pulled her to him. By the look in his eyes she had the distinct feeling that he intended to make love to her right there on the beach. "Justin," she gasped softly, "someone might see us."

The words got lost in his lips, in his breath, in his heat as he kissed her. His mouth was moving fervently on hers, his hand was stealing inside her bathing suit, cupping her naked breast, and Lauren was instantly, wildly aroused.

"Oh God," she moaned, "someone will see us." But the words were only a fainthearted attempt to stem the tidal wave of desire washing through her. She felt a sharp spasm in her stomach muscles as he worked his other hand inside her suit and cupped both her breasts, urging her toward him, caressing her roughly and murmuring in her ear.

"Tell me what you want," he breathed, and as the words seared through Lauren's consciousness she knew what she wanted. She wanted him, to make love with him, on the beach, *anywhere*.

Drawing back, staring into his eyes, she told him so.

He caught hold of her waist. "God, yes, I'm going to make love to you," he vowed, "but not here, Lauren, *not here*. I want you alone, I want it private—"

She tried to tell him that it didn't matter where they were, that she was crazy for him, aching for him, but the sudden tension in his posture, the strange lights in his eyes stopped her. He shook his head and pressed his hand to her mouth, confusing her with his hesitation.

"Wait," he whispered, and then suddenly, without warning, his body went rigid and his sensual murmurs became a low hiss. *"Be quiet."* He pulled her into his arms, holding her, paralyzed, listening.

"What is it?" she gasped.

In a flash of movement, he rolled her off him and into the sand, covering her with his body, cutting off her questions with the hand clamped over her mouth. "Be quiet, Lauren," he whispered. "I heard something."

She quieted, her heart throbbing.

He moved off her, crouching, stopping her as she tried to sit up. "Stay here. Let me find out what it was."

"It's probably someone from the party."

"No, the noise came from the trees behind us."

"But Justin, it could be anything, an animal—"

He hushed her and crept back toward the trees. Lauren watched him in a state of shock and confusion. It was probably one of the wild cats. Why did he assume there was some kind of danger? She sat up and crossed her arms, hugging herself, suddenly chilled by dissipating body heat. Moments ago, she'd been half-crazy with desire, so hot and breathless she would have made love right there on the beach. Now she felt like someone had thrown cold water in her face.

He was back, pulling her to her feet and talking to her before she'd fully registered his presence. "Lauren, there's an emergency. I've got to go. Can you get back to the castle all right?"

"An emergency?" She saw someone hovering behind him, a Bajan teenager half hidden in the shadows. "Justin, who is that?"

"It's okay. He's helping me." He drew her head back, his features urgent. "Look at me, Lauren, listen to me. There's something I have to take care of. I'm sorry, honest to God, I am, but that's all I can tell you for now."

She closed her eyes briefly as his lips brushed hers. When she opened them, he and the boy were disappearing into the trees.

The moke hit a rut and was airborne as it careened down a sharp incline and broke open the veil of darkness below. The road was a silver river, the car a streak of headlights, its engine whining at full force. Each collision of chassis with rutted road sent up an echoing wail of metal and springs. In the silent eyes of the jungle, they were an intrusion, this man, boy and machine, flying through the torpid night, a single unit of thrust and energy.

They approached a three-way fork, and the boy began gesturing, flailing his arms. "Go that way," he screamed over the engine, pointing northeast.

Justin let up on the accelerator and hit the brakes,

squirreling around the corner. The squeal of rubber tautened his nerves. He was driving too fast, and he knew it, feeding his premonition that the woman would vanish before he got there.

"Up ahead," the boy said, pointing out a sliver of blackness in the dense wall of trees and vegetation to their right. Justin spun the wheel and the headlights revealed an overgrown road. He switched off his lights and pulled onto it, negotiating the moke along hard-packed clay not much wider than a walking trail.

Monkeys shrieked and birds cawed above them, their signals drifting on the humid breezes. Unwilling to use his headlights and risk signaling their arrival, Justin relied on instinct and on the brilliance of the full moon to negotiate a path through the vines hanging in their path and the tree branches that clawed at them.

A half mile later the trail opened onto a tangled clearing. Set off to one side, nearly hidden by the overgrowth, was a small ramshackle hut, its one window yellowed with flickering candlelight.

Justin pulled the moke to a stop, cut the engine and caught the boy's arm, restraining him from scrambling out. "How do you know this woman?"

"She healed my mother of the fever," he said, trying to jerk away.

"And did she send the note you delivered to me at the castle?" The boy nodded. "Why?" Justin asked.

"She wanted to be sure you were the right man." Twisting free, he jumped from the moke and dashed into the hovel. Seconds later, he appeared in the window, signaling Justin with a wave of his hand.

Justin didn't see the woman when he entered. After the darkness, the hut's flickering light was so intense that all he could discern was a haze of tiny flames, row after row of candles, lined up along the floor, tiered on wall shelves. As his vision cleared, he saw the large jugs and jars, the hanging feathers, strung beads and snake bones. He knew enough about voodoo from his trips to Haiti and the other islands to recognize the paraphernalia.

A rattling sound made him reach for his knife.

"No!" The boy put his hand up. "It is her, Soodeen. She is here, over here."

Justin moved out of the glare of the candles and saw a tiny crone of a woman arising from a straw mat. She stared up at him, her spine a parenthetical curve, her face as wizened and gauzy as a dried leaf. She held some rocks in her hand, tiny polished agates, and she was working them with her fingers.

"Is she a *mambo*?" Justin asked the boy, using the Haitian name for a voodoo priestess.

"Mambo, voodoo, black magic," the woman scoffed quietly, her voice as knotted and grainy as old hemp. "I be no mambo, no magic-maker. I be old woman, sick woman."

Justin wasn't sure he believed her denial, but he wasn't going to risk alienating her for several reasons, including the fact that he needed her help. She was staring at him with eyes that pierced, as though all of her energy was concentrated there. Obsidian eyes, he thought, incongruous in her frail, withered frame.

"To you I am wretched and miserable, yes?" she asked, startling him with the question.

"No—"

"You can speak the truth." She smiled, a crackle of sound vibrating in her throat. "The old and the wretched have the best secrets."

"Perhaps you can help me then," Justin said, approaching her. "I'm searching for something—"

"I know who you be." Her eyes glittered like the rocks she was clicking in her hand. "And I know what you seek."

"Can you help me then? Will you?"

Suddenly she dropped the agates, or threw them to the floor. They made a terrible shattering sound, bouncing, popping and snapping as though they were alive. Justin heard the boy moan and turned to see him running from the hut.

"The thing you seek has spirits, evil spirits," the old woman rasped.

Justin's heart thudded. "No, it's just a ring, an antique ring."

She began swaying and weaving then, making a low, horrible sound. "It be cursed, that ring," she wheezed, her arms jerking and flapping like a decrepit bird trying to fly. "It seeks its other half, it seeks its lover."

Justin watched her, immobilized for a moment. He knew how to deal with tangible threats, but this? "I have the interlocking part," he said harshly, cutting through her moans. "I can put an end to the curse."

She let out a low wail and brought her hands up, shielding her face. "You find it, take it away? Off the island?"

"Yes, yes, I'll take it off the island."

She quieted then, still swaying, her hands at her throat. "All I know be this," she crooned. "On the third day the moon enters the Scorpion. That night the way be shown."

He recognized her words as some primitive form of astronomy. "What does that mean? Where is the ring now?"

"That ring be stolen from Sam Lord's castle—before me, before my mother and her mother. The thief, he die like an animal, ripped to shreds by demons." She looked up at him, her features skeletal and crumbling, but with a grip to them that was terrifying. "The thief, he break ring apart, separate the lovers, try to sell. That be the ring's curse."

"Where is the ring now?"

"His woman, she bring it back to castle, hide it there."

"Where? Where in the castle?"

She pointed a knotted finger toward the window. "When the moon turns green like the sea, follow its rays."

"But what the hell does that mean?" he pressed, frustrated by her evasiveness.

Turning from him, she began moaning again,

swaying, chanting something unintelligible. The candles in the hut flickered wildly and the door creaked open behind Justin.

"Come on!" the boy hissed, his eyes wide with fear. "We have to leave now."

"How do I get her to talk to me?" Justin said.

The boy shook his head frantically. "She won't. She's talking to the wise ones, the spirits. If you touch her now, they will enter your body through hers and you will go mad."

The woman shrieked and twirled. The boy darted from the doorway, his fear so palpable that Justin felt it, too.

A pulse beat sharply in Justin's throat. The woman's eyes were glazed and unseeing; her body was shuddering through some internal earthquake. She was in some kind of a trance and instinct told him not to interfere. He was also inclined to believe that she'd told him everything she knew. She had no reason not to, especially since she wanted the ring off the island. At least, he thought, she'd narrowed his search down to the castle. Shutting out her horrific wailing, he turned to the door, his mind on his next move.

Lauren sat curled up on the bed, sipping the Chambéryzette she'd ordered from room service. It was made from vermouth and the juice of wild strawberries and was delicious. But her mind wasn't on the wine, it was on the fiasco her vacation had become. I should catch the first flight out tomorrow morning, she thought, and end this craziness. Rene might call her a coward, but then Rene wasn't *here*, trapped on this sensual sauna bath of an island.

Lauren refilled her glass with the pale pink wine and sipped absently, aware that she'd already gone beyond her usual two-glass limit. It was just after midnight, and she was still badly shaken by the chaotic events of the evening, by Justin's abrupt departure. There was no doubt in her mind that she would have made love with him if they hadn't been interrupted. The erotic sensations were still swirling through her magically, as though they would never stop, like the infinite ripple effect of a rock tossed into a pond. But, strangely, even more powerful in her memory was that one moment of freedom when she knew she wanted him. She felt as though she'd opened a door and crossed over a threshold, as though she'd shed some protective covering. It had thrilled her then. It frightened her now.

She held the wineglass to her lips and took a long swallow. What's *happening* to me? she wondered. Her head was flooding her with warnings, all the same message: *Get off the island, get away from him.* If that weren't the same head that had been dissuading her from meaningful relationships all her adult life, she might have listened to it instantly. As it was, she simply wasn't sure. Did she have a real excuse to run away from him? Or would she be running from herself again, repeating the past? He'd left her for an emergency, but that wasn't an unpardonable sin in most people's books. He hadn't hurt her, unless you counted burning desire as a form of torture. He'd even rescued her once.

Setting her glass down on the nightstand, Lauren sighed heavily and fell back against the bed's pillows. She had questions, so many questions, and no answers. Her eyes drifted shut automatically and she stretched out on the bed. She was tired, she realized, bone-tired and aching in places she'd forgotten all about.

She dozed for some time, aware in her semi-conscious state that the light was still on and that she was wearing the bathing suit she'd worn to the beach party. She was also aware that she hadn't the energy to do anything about those things, or even to move. Her muscles felt heavy and leaden. Her head felt fuzzy and feverishly hot. I've either drunk too much or been drugged, she thought, smiling drowsily as she remembered her last phone conversation with Rene.

Finally, hours later, she reached up to turn off the light and sank back into the darkness and into dreams that swept her toward the sun and sacrificed her to its incendiary heat. She tossed restlessly, captive to the sweet, burning torture that engulfed her, scorched by the flames and crying out a name, Justin's name.

She awoke once in the dead of night and saw that her room was ablaze with moonlight. Stark white and blinding, it flashed off the wall mirror and electrified the carved monkey's green eyes. Lying in a pool of reflected light, she tried to rouse herself and couldn't. The monkey's features threw grotesque shadows, elongated and menacing, and its eyes were glaring at her, a bone-chilling glare...but she couldn't move.

She heard the soft meow of a cat somewhere in the

distance. Rolling to her side, she reached for the lamp on the nightstand, and her fingers clinked against glass. The wine goblet rocked a little, splashing wine on her hand and filling the room with the scent of strawberries. *Find the cat,* she thought, sensing somehow that it was important, but unable to shake off her lethargy. She sank back into the pillows, dragged down by the soft, black clutches of sleep.

Someone was knocking on the door in Lauren's dream, softly at first and then more insistently. "Come in," she murmured, her lashes fluttering drowsily. Through gauzy shards of sunlight, she saw someone enter her room and wondered if she was still dreaming.

"Your breakfast, ma'am."

Feeling the feathery tickle of her own hair draping her face, Lauren wrinkled her nose. "Breakfast?" Still not sure this wasn't a dream, she brushed the hair away and squinted her eyes to the silhouette of a man holding a tray at the end of her bed. "What time is it?" she asked.

"Time to get up, you lazy wench."

Lauren opened her eyes completely.

The waiter walked through the hazy barrier of sunlight and into her visual frame of reference. Yes, she was dreaming. "Justin, what are you doing here? In that white jacket? With that tray?"

"I needed work," he said, wry amusement in his smile as he set the tray on her bed. "What are you doing in that bathing suit?"

She glanced down and automatically pulled the spread over herself. The suit was more revealing than her nightgowns. "I guess I fell asleep this way."

Watching her steadily, he pulled off the cropped white jacket and tossed it on the foot of the bed. "Explain something to me," he said, approaching her. "Why do you feel the need to cover yourself when I've already seen you naked?"

"Maybe that's why." Lauren tugged the spread tighter as he sat on the bed, his hip brushing her thigh. He was wearing faded denims that fit him better than pants had a right to and a loose white cotton shirt with the sleeves rolled up. "I wasn't totally naked," she said, as though that distinction made a difference.

He glanced at the bottle of Chambéryzette on the nightstand and the spilled wine. "What did you do? Tie one on last night?"

"Of course not," she said, a shade defensively. "Not that I didn't have reason to—after being mauled and then thrown on the sand and discarded."

He laughed softly. "Mauled? Who leapt onto who's lap?"

"A gentleman wouldn't…" She raised an eyebrow and let the dangling sentence speak for itself.

"A gentleman wouldn't drag that bedspread off you and take possession of your sweet body right here on this bed, either." His eyes sparkled.

Lauren grabbed hold of the spread with both hands and shook her head. "You're not dragging anything off me, Mister, not without an explanation."

Again Justin had to fight down the desire that rose inside him. Low laughter in his throat, he stood and stared down at her, wishing he could do exactly what he'd threatened. Instead, dammit, he was going to do exactly what he'd come here to do even if it killed him. He was going to give her what she wanted—an explanation. Walking to the window, he glanced out, took a long, hard breath, and then he settled himself on the sill. "Yesterday I told you I was a treasure hunter. That's part of the reason I came to Barbados."

"There's treasure on this island?"

"Probably more than anyone ever dreamed of, but what I'm looking for isn't buried in the ground or at the bottom of the Caribbean. It's hidden somewhere, maybe even in this castle." He stopped himself as she sat up a little, still clutching the spread to her. She was curious, but how much could he safely tell her? How much could he risk so that she would understand that he had little choice in what he was going to do? "That boy last night had some vital information for me, and I had to follow it up."

"I see."

No, you don't see, he thought, turning to stare out the window. "What I'm doing has a certain level of secrecy attached to it, Lauren."

"Secrecy? Are you an agent or something?"

"No, this is a personal mission. That's all I can tell you right now." He turned back to her, sobering, aware that he owed her more than he was giving her. The possibility that he would have to hurt her before this was over had been haunting him. "I know all this sounds like something out of a spy novel," he said, clearing his throat of its huskiness, "and if that makes you uneasy…if you don't want to see me again, just say so."

Not see him? Lauren's breathing went shallow. He'd just confirmed all her fears about him. He was hiding something. He *did* have secrets. And now he was giving her the perfect out. Her body's response was sharp and immediate, a tightening in her belly, a fuzzy ache at the back of her throat.

"On the other hand," he said, exhaling, "if you're feeling adventurous—well, adventurous enough to put up with a guy like me—then I've got something special in mind for tonight."

"Special?"

He picked up the tray, set it over her legs and pointed to the small linen envelope set against the crystal bud vase. It had Lauren's name written on it.

She opened it, her fingers unsteady. Inside she found a beautiful engraved invitation to the Castle Dinner. Her pulse quickened. She'd heard of the Castle Dinner. It *was* special, a black-tie affair, served in the elegant, private dining room downstairs for a dozen couples only, eight courses of haute cuisine and the finest wines.

She looked up and caught him in an unguarded moment of expectation. "Will you come with me?" he asked.

His steady gaze awakened the response that she'd come to expect when their eyes met, the need to breathe deeply, the quick and beautiful moment of near pain. *How does a woman say no to this man?* she wondered.

Eight

On the third day, the moon enters the Scorpion. That night the way be shown. Justin repeated the phrase in his mind as he stared up at the heavens. The moon hung huge in the early-evening sky, a globe so full and bright that its craters and waterless seas could be seen by the naked eye. Was this that prophesied night? he wondered. The palms and banyans swaying above him whispered *yesss* as he continued his walk in the castle gardens.

Dressed in black tie for the castle dinner, he'd arrived early and used the time to survey the grounds and the various entrances to the castle. Now, satisfied that he'd learned everything he could, he was simply appreciating both the May evening and the Georgian mansion for their unrivaled splendor…and wondering what secrets they might surrender before the night was through.

A flickering motion caught his eye, drawing his attention to the castle's second story. In the southeast corner, he saw a woman at the open balcony window, beautiful and ethereal, her gossamer dress floating in the air currents.

Caught in the sight, he thought of the fanciful stories of hauntings and ghosts, of Lucy's appearances on the balcony. The woman he saw now was misty and motionless, a moonlit apparition. Who is she? he asked, and all at once, the night and the wind and his mind whispered *Lauren*. As she disappeared from the window, Justin strode toward the castle steps.

Lauren stepped back from the balcony window, the champagne chiffon of her floor-length gown swirling around her. Having no idea that Justin had seen her, she left her room and approached the staircase to the main hall. She'd thought of nothing else but this evening all day. And now, wearing the dress she'd found in the shop on the hotel grounds, and with her hair done up and her spirits soaring, she felt magical, a woman made of soft breezes and starlight.

Would Justin be here yet? she wondered, hesitating at the banister. They'd planned to meet at the predinner cocktail party in the drawing room. Gathering up her dress, she descended the stairs, reached the second landing and saw him waiting at the bottom. Her heart faltered. With his sunswept blond hair and dark tan, he looked magnificent in evening clothes. She'd never seen a man so handsome.

His eyes told her he was equally struck. She wasn't

sure she'd ever seen him awed, or even caught off guard, and the moment gave her such a swell of joy that she hesitated on the stairs. He held his hand out as though he couldn't wait a moment longer to touch her. Oh God, she thought. This *is* the night. It didn't matter to her at all that he had secrets, or that he might be involved in something dangerous. *Everyone* had secrets. *Life was dangerous.* She just wanted to be with him, intimately, passionately. Given the choice, she would have sacrificed even this elegant dinner to be alone with him for a few minutes.

Justin read the desire in her eyes, in her smile, in the breathy shiver of her décolletage. Her dress's deeply cut bodice buoyed her lush breasts in a way that made his chest tighten. She could have been a woman out of the baroque past, a Regency debutante, a French courtesan...

He took her hand, felt the delicate bones, the heat of her flesh, and a sensation caught him deep in his vitals, a bolt of lightning—tiny, white-hot and intensely pleasurable. God, he thought, I can't wait any longer for this woman. I'm not even sure I can make it through dinner.

They were looking at each other, both on the brink of suggesting something forbidden, when a Bajan head-waiter in tails and white gloves announced dinner.

"Dinner," Lauren said.

"Dinner," Justin agreed. "Are you hungry?"

The waiter announced again, staring at them so imperiously that Lauren nodded reluctantly.

The meal was a lavish affair, eight courses beginning with a clear turtle soup laced with sherry. Lobster in champagne sauce followed by lime sorbet to clear the palate, and each course was accompanied by a superb Grand Cru wine.

It was all artfully prepared and tempting, but Lauren was too nervous to eat much. With Justin beside her, his eyes full of sexy intrigue, it was difficult to concentrate on food, no matter how sumptuous the meal. "I thought you were hungry?" he bent and whispered to her at one point. Her answer was a smile and a meaningful glance at the slab of beef Wellington growing cold on *his* plate.

A delicious tension had been building between them all evening. They were sharply aware of each other and, at the same time, awash in their own private thoughts, anticipating the evening ahead, when they would finally be alone. Neither could concentrate on anything else, not even the romantic tales of Sam Lord and Lucy the castle's manager-host regaled them with all evening.

When the last course was finally cleared, their host suggested the women might like to freshen up before joining the men in the drawing room for cognac.

"I'll be right back," Lauren assured Justin, thrilled by his reluctance to let her go.

She never reached the ladies' room. Trailing behind the other women, her mind on other things, she took the wrong hallway, doubled back and was snagged by a hand flashing out of a doorway as she passed. Spun around and tugged into a darkened room, she caught a glimpse of her assailant's features in the moonlight. "Justin!"

"Surprise," he said, laughing softly. His hands were warm and firm on her arms, his eyes brilliant.

Lauren's body had stopped spinning, but her head hadn't. Light with shock, she pressed her palms to his chest to steady herself. The defined muscularity and warmth of his pectorals were evident even through his clothing. "I guess this means we're skipping the cognac?" was all she could manage.

"Not necessarily." He covered one of her hands, brought it to his mouth and kissed her fingertips. "I had some sent up to your room." His breath rushed hot over exquisitely sensitive nerve endings.

A pulse stitched erratically in Lauren's throat.

"Oh…I see."

A silence closed around them as they gazed at each other, snared in a web of quickening heartbeats and rocketing excitement. He kissed her fingertips again, and Lauren felt a sinking warmth in her belly. She knew by the look in his eyes if they didn't leave this storage room—or whatever it was—soon, they might not leave at all. "Suddenly, I'm in the mood for some cognac," she said softly.

He exhaled his agreement and caught hold of her hand. "We won't be missed," he said under his breath as they left the room and started down the hallway. "I told our host I was coming down with something, a fever."

Looking up, she caught a glitter of sexual heat beneath the irony in his eyes.

"The fever part is true," he said.

A small group of late-registering guests turned to stare at them as they walked through the check-in area. Justin greeted them so pointedly, he embarrassed them into looking away, and then he tugged Lauren's hand, and they bolted up the stairway to the second floor, Lauren holding up her skirt and laughing. She slipped on the top step, just a momentary loss of balance in the heat of their escape, but it was enough to throw her against the mahogany banister. She flinched as the sharp scrollwork bit into her hip, and then she shook her head and laughed it all away, the pain, the concern in Justin's eyes. "I'm fine," she insisted, "it's only a bruise."

They both grew quiet when they got to her room. A tray of Cognac and two balloon glasses awaited them on the writing desk by the window. Lauren hesitated by the door while Justin walked to it and tipped up the bottle to read the label. She suddenly felt self-conscious, watching him, wondering what came next. Would he open the Cognac? Would they go through the ritual of toasting, drinking, pretending not to be in breathless need of each other? As often as they'd been together, teetering on the brink of intimacy, this moment felt incredibly awkward to Lauren.

"Courvoisier," Justin said, setting the bottle down. He hesitated, running his thumb along the label. "Shall I open it?"

"No, don't," she said, a thread of urgency shimmering somewhere beneath the words.

He turned to her expectantly.

Aware of his eyes on her, Lauren caught a glimpse of herself in the mirror of the armoire, and the sight was riveting. For a moment she wasn't at all certain it was her own reflection she was seeing. The woman in the mirror was flushed, and her eyes were sparkling. Alluringly disarrayed, her upswept hair glowed with golden fire, and silky wisps floated around her face. Reaching up, Lauren touched a tendril of hair, just to be sure. Something was happening to her, something odd and compelling. Her heart rate was erratic, fast and fluttery, and then, as she turned back to Justin, it slowed to a heavier, almost painful beat. Even from this distance she could see it, that riveting blue flame in his eyes.

"I saw you earlier tonight, on the balcony," he said, hesitating, a whispering roughness in his breath. "You could have been the White Lady the islanders talk about."

The words swept through Lauren's consciousness. *The White Lady...Lucy, the ghost whose spells made lovers irresistible to each other.*

Justin's silent gaze was moving up her body like a slow spotlight, touching her breasts, her mouth, her eyes. "God, you're beautiful."

Lauren's heart somersaulted. No man had ever spoken to her like that before...oh, the words, yes. She'd heard those words before, but never in that grainy tone of voice or with such undisguised ardor.

They were a whole room apart: he at the desk, she by the door, and all she could think about was how long it was going to take him to get to her. Her pulse pounded with that question. Everything else was answered. They would make love, that was as inevitable as the sunrise; and yes, they would be wild and beautiful, like untamed animals, urgent in their need. She knew that, too. It was the way he would start it that had her half crazy with wondering. Would he ask her to undress for him again? Dear God, would he ask that?

"Lauren," he said harshly, "Lauren, come here."

She took a step and felt herself trembling. He wanted her to come to him...and she couldn't. Her legs were water.

He held out one hand to her. With the other he undid the black silk tie he wore and left it hanging loose around his neck. Staring at her, a stirring need in his eyes, he worked free the top button of his shirt.

Lauren closed her eyes for an instant as a sliding sensation deep in her belly riveted her awareness. It was thrilling and disorienting, a purely physical thing, like stepping off an embankment and not finding the ground underneath you. When she opened her eyes, he was still there, across the room, standing in the streaming moonlight.

"Lauren, don't make me come and get you," he said, his voice low and ragged. "I don't trust myself to do that."

Her breath caught as the sensation inside her spiked. It was like free-fall, like plummeting through space. He seemed a continent away as she started toward him, her steps jerky and hesitant, her body buffeted by conflicting urges. One part of her was unnaturally frightened by the flare in his eyes. Another part of her was wild to be in his arms.

She stopped just beyond his reach, wondering what would happen to her when he touched her. In that instant of hesitation, she averted her eyes, but she couldn't shut out her own hammering heart, or the physical grip in his voice when he spoke.

"Take down your hair, Lauren," he said, a dangerous tautness in his voice. "Take it down for me."

She reached up to take out the pins, and he caught hold of her wrist and pulled her to him, a sound in his throat like a tortured groan. She gasped as he turned her face up to him. "What the hell are you doing to me?" he said. "I've never been crazy with a woman. I've never been like this before." He held her face with both hands, bathing her with the heat of his breath. When he kissed her, it was with inhuman control, barely touching her lips with his, and yet burning her with his passion, thrilling her with the low, whispering ferocity in his voice. "Do you know what I am with you?" he said. "I'm driven, obsessed. I've never wanted a woman this badly."

He caught her by the waist and drew her up against him, kissing her roughly, deeply, hunger spilling over from his need. She didn't try to resist; she couldn't. Something profound was happening inside her, a flow of crystalline light through her veins. His tongue penetrated the barrier of her lips and a liquid sensation swept her, hot and sweet, drenching her limbs, draining her of resistance. She was breathless and dizzy in its wake.

She was astonished and grateful and terrified. Did other people feel this way? she wondered, the odd thought darting through her delirium—this transfiguring fire that was melting her will and her bones?

Justin's voice broke through her immersion. "Touch me, Lauren," he whispered. "Put your arms around me."

She responded instinctively, running her hands along his back, marveling at the heat and sheer tactile pleasure of his rippling muscles. They were a river of granite, hard one moment, fluid the next. She touched his hip, and his response mesmerized her. A sensual rattle from deep in his chest brought back visions of the golden animal, beautiful and capable of savagery.

He broke the kiss, his hands rigid on her throat, his thumbs caressing her jawline. "You're trembling everywhere. Am I frightening you?"

"Yes," she said, and then, from out of nowhere, an unsteady smile touched her lips. "But you're thrilling me, too." She reached out, touched his jawline with her fingers. "And I like that part."

"Oh, my God," he said, a kind of pain in his laughter. "You're a lunatic."

"Moon madness."

He shrugged off his jacket and flung it onto the chair.

Lauren sucked in her breath, sure he was going to rip off the rest of his clothes. Instead, he looked at her for a flurry of seconds, and then, with a slow, sweet rigidness in his touch, he eased his fingers into the silky tangle of her hair. "Do you believe in ghosts?" he asked.

"I believe in it all," she said softly, echoing his own words, "ghosts, magic, spells. If you don't believe, it doesn't exist."

"Then believe this." His fingers contracted in her hair as he drew her closer. "I have been in need of you, Lauren, painful need of you for days. I am under some kind of spell, and you're going to set me free—tonight."

The words gave Lauren a sudden and startling glimpse of the power a woman could have over a man. Breathy laughter quivered in her throat. "Suppose I do…set you free. What are you going to do for me?"

"This," he said. Staring deep into her eyes, he began to draw up her dress, his fingers grazing her thighs. The chiffon fabric floated on her skin.

"Justin! What are you doing?"

"Thrilling you. Is it working?"

"Lord, yes."

Lauren had skipped nylons because of the heat, and the feel of his hands on her bare skin was riveting. Within seconds he'd slid the dress above her thighs. Her stomach tightened as the breezes touched her heated flesh, and the light stroke of his hands filled her head with forbidden fantasies.

The sensations were so sharp she found it difficult to breathe, and that dazzling liquid heat was spreading through her muscles again, heating her imagination, drenching her with lassitude. "Oh, Justin, I don't know about this. Maybe you could thrill me a little less?"

His eyes were blue fire. "No mercy," he warned, his voice husky and rustling with sensuality.

He wadded the dress in his fists, tugging her back to his lips. Lauren breathed a soft cry of pleasure as he released the chiffon and cupped her buttocks, pulling her up against him. His hardened shaft pressed into her belly and sent up flares of fiery sweetness. The deep muscles of her stomach pulled tight in anticipation.

"I could die from this," she gasped.

"But you won't," he said. "I promise."

He slid his hands down the back of her thighs and gripped her legs. Lifting her, wrapping her legs around his waist, he carried her to the bed. "I have a raging need to be inside you," he said, lowering her, letting her fall back.

A craziness came over Lauren as she sprawled on the bed, her arms flung out just as she'd fantasized the night she'd kissed him. She was gripped with the sweetest, wildest frenzy, possessed by a radiance that blazed through her body and ignited in her loins. The pleasure of it was unbearable. Gasping softly, she reached for the man standing over her.

He sank down, reaching up her body to her breasts, cupping them, urging her up to him. "We may *both* die from this," he breathed against her mouth.

He reached behind her to unzip her dress, but she caught his hand and brought it to her mouth, kissing his fingers. "There isn't time for that," she said, a tremor of anguish in her voice. She couldn't bear to have him undress her, to arouse her any more. She was already aroused to the point of pain. She found his hardness through the fabric of his pants and pressed her hand along its length.

She felt his stomach muscles contract, heard the hard, concussive breath he took, as though someone had knocked the wind out of him. And then everything happened so fast she could barely catch her breath. He dropped her back down and moved above her, stripping off her panties, opening her legs. She was caught in the fire of his eyes, barely aware as he released his zipper and moved between her legs.

Suddenly the wondrous heat of him pressed at the juncture of her thighs. A silent cry ripped though her body as he penetrated her, coaxing her tautened muscles into accepting him and then driving into her softness with an anguished groan. He lifted himself on powerful arms and moved above her, filling her with his male power, touching all the way to her womb with his strokes.

It was fast and frenzied and beautiful. Lauren moaned with pleasure, astonished at the glorious pressure building inside her and terrified he might stop before the tension was released. His thrusts rocked her body into a sweet, aching bundle of tender moans and exquisitely sensitized nerves. He *was* thrilling her to death, she thought, and then a shuddering tremor took her unexpectedly, forcing a cry to her lips and hot tears to her eyes. The power of it was incredible, shattering. Another tremor shook her and another, like beautiful bursts of music, like the clash of cymbals. In the wonder of it all, she gasped and sobbed and reached for him, calling out his name.

"I'm here," he said, gathering her up into his arms,

rolling with her, holding her, their limbs hopelessly entangled, his body still deeply within hers. "I'm here, Lauren, beautiful Lauren. I'm here."

He hesitated while she quieted, brushing her tears, kissing her with such infinite tenderness, and all the while moving inside her, rocking her to a new rhythm until finally she felt herself tightening again, arcing along a current of light toward some wondrous landscape. Through the soaring joy, she could feel inner muscles tightening rhythmically around him, could see him buck back and arch, a look of wonder and agony gripping his face. A guttural cry shook him as he dropped.

"Justin?" she breathed, and this time she gathered him into her arms, pressing her lips to his temple, his hair. Listening to his soft gasps, she was exultant that she could bring him such pleasure. Her heart swelled and squeezed tight inside her. So this, she thought, the tears welling hot in her eyes, is what it's all about.

Nine

"Now that we've made love, maybe we should take our clothes off and get into bed?" Justin suggested, kissing Lauren's collarbone where it jutted delicately above her breast. They were lying on the bed, still dazed and dreamy a half hour after the lovemaking, Lauren's dress bunched up underneath her, Justin's shirt pulled free, his pants a mass of wrinkles.

Lauren roused herself from his arms and laughed softly. "Will you look at that," she said, raising a foot and pointing to her high-heeled sandals. "I've still got my shoes on!"

"Couldn't be helped," he said wryly, kissing her chin. "One of us was in a hurry."

"Oh, and I guess you weren't?" She stared into his twinkling eyes and was swept by a wave of emotion so strong, she actually flushed with it. "Next time, no short cuts," she warned, covering her sudden vulnerability. "Undress me down to my toes, hear. Whoops!" she cried as he rolled her over onto her side and began to unzip her.

"The hell with next time—" he lifted her hair and nipped her earlobe "—do it now, that's my motto."

Justin felt her shiver under his hands as he slowly stripped the delicate dress from her body. Stroking her legs with his fingertips, he eased the gossamer material off her, and watched the spark of desire ignite in her eyes. He removed her shoes and tossed them onto the chair. Totally naked, she was so exquisite he was aroused again immediately. His excitement built as he pulled off his own clothes and saw her watching him, her eyes dilating rapidly as he stepped out of his pants and kicked them away. He'd always kept in shape, but her breathless scrutiny made him suddenly aware of his own body, of his own arousal.

"You're staring," he said.

"*You're* beautiful."

He grinned through a twist of desire. "I think that's my line."

"I borrowed it," she said, laughing softly.

Her eyes were so smoky and sexy and droopily lashed, he wondered how he'd ever held himself back with this woman. Her legs were miles long, her breasts high and full, their silky weight, their softness, a vivid memory. He could still feel her in his hands! It was only as he lay down beside her that he noticed the bruise, a ribbon of blue-black on her hip.

"Did I do that?" he asked, looking at her.

She shook her head. "The stairway, when I tripped and fell against the banister."

"Looks like you need the witch doctor." He kissed the tender spot on her hip, feathering it with butterfly touches of his lips and reaching up at the same time to cup her breast. He sank his fingers into her buttery flesh, and she arched up, whimpering with a soft, shocked sound as he excited her nipple with his thumb and brought it to a state of tautness.

Justin knew all about the sweet torment she was feeling. It was the same throbbing tension he had deep in his loins, a pleasure so intense he had to fight demons to keep it from escalating.

He concentrated on arousing her, on kissing and caressing every creamy inch of her body, and when he'd finished, he rolled her onto her stomach and discovered the sloping curve of her lower back, the taut, sweet rise of her buttocks. By the time he turned her over and spread her legs, she was gasping and begging him to enter her. Not yet, he thought, his stomach muscles seizing up in protest, *not quite yet.*

He stretched alongside her, drawing her up to him, kissing and hushing her with murmurous words. When she'd calmed a little, he trailed his hand up her thigh and found the silky heat between her legs, caressing it with his fingers. She moaned, her body convulsing as though his touch had sent a shock wave through her. She was so damn delicate there and so hot with desire, he felt her shudder rebound through him. The fiery ache in his loins told him he couldn't wait much longer, but there was something he had to do, something he couldn't resist. Lowering himself, he replaced his probing fingers with his lips and his tongue and rediscovered her silkiness. She responded with motion and sound, her body bucking against him, her cries so sharp they pierced him.

He entered her just as she began to spasm and cry and soar toward ecstasy. Feeling as though he would come apart with desire, he drove into her slowly and deeply, rigid with the control it took, letting her melt around him, letting her cry out her pleasure and rock him with her sweet, pulsing thrusts. He groaned in his throat as her climax truly began, her heat sheathing him and the delicate flutter of feminine muscles caressing him like wing strokes.

His release, when it came, was mind altering. Starting in his throat, tumbling down his body, it caught him like raging white water and swept him along with it, pounding him, pummeling him with the most agonizing pleasure he'd ever felt.

Moments later, or hours, he wasn't sure, he awoke as though from a dream and felt her curled alongside his body. Gathering her in closer, he reveled in the warmth of her skin, the soft thud of her heartbeat against his ribs. Pressing his lips to her hair, taking in its clean, fragrant scent, he marveled on how different the female body was from the male—on how soft she was, how fragile her limbs compared to his.

It was several seconds before he began to register her shallow breathing. Alerted, he picked up a tiny shudder, a swallowed sigh. "Lauren, what is it?"

He brought her face up and saw crumpled features and eyes full of unshed tears.

"You're crying?"

She shook her head, obviously embarrassed, but her chin trembled and a tear brimmed over. "I—yes, sorry—"

Her voice was so soaked with emotion, he felt his heart plummet. "Sorry about what? What's wrong?"

"I don't know—" She shook her head, the words sighing out on a wave of self-reproach. "Oh, that's not true. I *do* know, but I'm not sure I can explain it."

"Try."

She looked away then, as though acutely self-conscious of the emotions trembling through her. "I never knew it could be like this—" Her voice broke, and she shook her head. "I know how incredible that must sound coming from a thirty-three-year-old woman, but I never knew *anything* could be like this."

"Hey," he soothed, "it's okay. You don't have to—"

She drew in a breath, collecting herself, and finally she looked up at him. "Yes...I do have to."

It seemed to take her a moment to summon the rest of her control, but when she did, the words came out measured, with only a hint of the halting emotion behind them. "I know it sounds crazy," she told him, "but in a way this was the first time for me. Not in the technical sense, I've made love before, but this was the first time I've ever…participated." Her eyes, suddenly sparkling with tears, asked him to understand. "Do you know what it's like to feel like a spectator during the most intimate act two human beings can engage in? Do you have any idea?"

Yeah, he had an idea. He'd had a few spectator experiences himself. "Sure, I do," he said, brushing away her tears. He gave her a tender kiss and a reassuring smile, but when she couldn't quite smile back he knew it was something more. It was different with her, a deeper issue. He ran his finger along the same collarbone he'd kissed earlier and tapped her lower lip tenderly. "Lauren, I've never met a woman who participates like you do."

The smile she hadn't quite managed before seemed to break inside her now. It trembled on her mouth, glowing through her tears. She's *beautiful*, he thought, wondering if he should tell her what she'd done to him, how profoundly she'd affected him. He decided against it for a reason he didn't quite understand. It had to do with the hollow sensation in his stomach and the odd weakness in his heartbeat.

"Do you know that you've changed my life?" she said, her voice unsteady with emotion. She touched his face, and his heart bucked.

He immediately regretted his startled expression. She reacted defensively, averting her eyes, shaking her head and laughing as though she'd done it again, embarrassed them both. "Don't ever take a woman who suffers from moon madness too seriously," she warned him, a catch in her voice.

She was obviously hurt and trying hard not to be. All Justin could think about was finding some way to bring that radiant smile back to her face. He took her in his arms, conflict eating him up inside. Something had happened between them tonight, but he knew it wasn't possible to pursue it, or anything else with her, not without starting something he couldn't finish, not without saying things he had no right to say.

"Lauren, I'm sorry," he whispered, tilting her head up and kissing the moistness around her eyes, whispering soft things to her. He couldn't help himself. He had this compelling urge to be tender with her beyond anything he'd ever felt before. "You caught me off guard, that's all."

He lifted her into his arms, holding her as he got off the bed, pulled back the covers and deposited her inside. When he slipped in beside her, she burrowed into his arms, pressing herself against him and snuggling her head into the curve of his shoulder.

His heart beat heavily with the things he couldn't say to her, with the emotions he felt but didn't fully understand. And finally, abruptly, he cut off all thought, as though he'd slammed a mental door. Get some sleep, he told himself harshly, knowing that all his gut-wrenching conflict was futile. He had only a few hours left with her at best.

The moonlight awoke him from a restless sleep, its glare so harsh he had to shield his eyes for a moment to get his bearings. Next to him, her back to the window,

Lauren was deep in peaceful slumber, her head tucked into the pillow. He checked the clock and saw that it was 2:00 a.m., an hour sooner than he'd told himself to awake.

The light streaming in the window was blinding. It flashed off a wall mirror, hit the armoire and ricocheted around the room. Squinting, Justin tried to figure out what was different about the stream, and as his eyes adjusted, he discerned the thin laser of green light.

Careful not to wake Lauren, he slipped out of the bed and walked to the wall mirror, spotting the source of the laser immediately. Emerald light streaked from the oddly faceted glass eyes of a monkey's head carved into the wooden frame of a wall mirror. Its trajectory was the armoire against the wall. Justin's pulse accelerated as he repeated the Bajan woman's second clue in his head. *When the moon turns green like the sea, follow its rays.*

He dressed quickly, silently, and then he searched the armoire from top to bottom, checking for false sides and compartments. Finding none, he eased the wardrobe away from the wall and felt along its back. His foot snagged something on the floor against the wall, a chink in the molding. A crackling sound froze him in place. He listened a moment, making sure he hadn't awakened Lauren, and then he checked along the wall. Something gave beneath his hands. Pressing his foot to the molding again, he watched a narrow, five-foot door swing open.

Damn, he thought, *damn*, this is it! He crouched,

slipped inside, cutting away cobwebs as thick as fish netting, and found himself on the top landing of a stairway. Its rotting wooden steps descended into blackness. A secret passageway to the dungeon, he reasoned, or to the underground tunnel that Sam Lord reputedly used to haul back loot from the shipwrecks.

A skittering sound caught his attention. He dug a penlight out of an inner pocket of his jacket and flashed it down the stairs, catching a momentary glint of a cat's eyes in its glare. One of the feral cats, undoubtedly. The dungeon was probably crawling with them.

Flashing the penlight up and down the stairway, satisfied that he was alone, he turned back and saw the laser piercing the darkness. The emerald beam shot through the door's narrow opening, pinpointing a wooden plank on the opposite wall of the landing. If the old woman was right, the ring was hidden somewhere in that wall.

Soundlessly, he returned to the bedroom, found some hotel notepaper and a pen on Lauren's dresser. She stirred as he began to write, and he hesitated, wondering what he would do if she woke, wondering if he could risk telling her.

She turned and reached toward the empty side of the bed, murmuring his name as though she knew he was gone. But her eyes never opened, and a moment later, she'd curled up into herself and was quiet again.

Staring at the blank paper that was to be a goodbye note, Justin found he couldn't write it. Fool, he thought, scribbling down a message that he knew could ultimately have dangerous consequences for him, perhaps even for her. Damn fool. He tossed the folded note on her dresser, grabbed his jacket and strode toward the passageway door.

Once inside, Justin retrieved the metal probe and lock pick he'd stashed in inner pockets of his jacket. He extended the probe's antenna, directed it toward the point of light and felt no reaction. Moving it up and down the wall, he anticipated the pull when the dowserlike instrument detected metal. Tension simmered in his gut. No reaction anywhere. Apparently, the old woman's clues were so much superstitious jibberish. He exhaled in sheer frustration. He'd come too far, risked too much to fail now.

He'd begun to comb the wall again when he noticed a small hole just above the laser's green light. Something had hung there once. He felt along the area with his fingers and found a tiny, sharp splinter of glass embedded in the wood. Or a mirror? An idea struck him. It was farfetched, but it was all he had. He slipped back into Lauren's bedroom, returned to the passageway with her hand mirror and broke the glass into several small pieces. Holding a fragment to the wall where the laser hit, he watched it bounce light down the stairway to the opposite wall. He quickly dug little grooves in the wood, affixed the mirror and followed its trajectory, pointing the probe's antenna at the new target. Still no reaction. He tried it again, affixing mirrors down the stairway, and bouncing light with no success until finally the emerald laser targeted a plank at the bottom of the stairway that had a large ugly knot midway up from its base.

The metal probe jerked in his grip as he approached. Instantly, he fished the pick from his pocket and began to pry the plank free. At the first wrench of pressure, the knot popped out, and the hole it left was just large enough to slip a hand through. Justin flashed the penlight inside, scanned the two-foot-square space and saw nothing but thick cobwebs and mounds of dust and grime. He reached in, probing in the near corners that couldn't be seen by the eye. Finally, his fingers hit something metallic buried in the gritty debris. It felt like a small tin box.

His heart thudding, he worked the box loose from its prison of encrusted grime—over a century's worth if the box held what he thought it did. Once he'd freed it, he grasped it in his hand and eased his fist back through the knothole. Shaking off the loose dust, he dug through the corrosion with the pick, pried open the box's lid and flashed the penlight again to see what he had. The antique gold ring's emerald-cut stone glinted like the precious gem it was, a smoky water sapphire. *Good God*, he'd found it. A weakness washed over him, sheer unadulterated relief, but he knew he couldn't afford that yet. He had to get the ring off the island.

He was securing the box and his equipment in an inner jacket pocket when he heard a sound behind him. He froze instinctively, then turned, flashing the penlight, expecting to see Lauren, or the cat. Instead, his light stopped on a scarred, one-eyed face hanging as though suspended in the darkness. The man he'd confronted at The Scarab bolted into action, hurtling at him. Justin dropped the light and kicked, connecting hard, aware as he drove his foot into the man's gut that a second assailant was coming at him from behind.

Lauren awoke slowly the next morning, a pleasant exhaustion tugging her back down into sleep every time she floated toward consciousness. Finally, shaking off the grogginess, she forced herself to sit up, and the effort brought a grimace of discomfort. Tender and stiff all over, she touched the bruise on her hip and winced. The witch doctor's magic hadn't worked this time, she thought, glancing at the empty space next to her and noticing that Justin was gone. *Gone?* Where was he?

The room held no trace of him. If it hadn't been for her own clothing scattered around the room and the tenderness she felt in certain places, she might have thought last night was an erotic dream.

Where had he gone? she wondered, the question bringing with it a spark of anxiety. She could feel doubts stirring inside her, curling, demanding recognition. "You will *not* do this to yourself, Lauren Cambridge," she said. "He's off getting coffee and the morning paper—or something." She settled back into the pillows, determined not to let herself ruin the rare mood she was in. The night they'd shared together had been too beautiful, too special to clutter it up with misgivings.

She smiled, remembering the frantic, erotic quality

of their lovemaking, remembering how he'd brought tears to her eyes with his unexpected gentleness. Her heart tightened as she thought about how he'd held her, rocked her, brushed away her tears.

In the next moments, a truth came to her, simple, undeniable. She could so easily love a man like him. She closed her eyes, experiencing the power of that declaration. In the course of knowing him, he'd brought her in touch with feelings she hadn't felt since childhood. Last night, he'd reminded her of even deeper feelings, the passion for attachment, the cry for belonging. Other people took love so much for granted. To Lauren, it was a brand-new and precious thing, a miracle.

Savoring the feelings, she wondered how she'd managed so long without them and why she'd been so frightened of them. Decisions made in childhood weren't easily revised, she decided. They were deep and rooted in unreasoning emotion. It took courage to move through them. It took a good friend like Rene to help you see that it was time to change; it took a man like Justin to make you want to. Opening her eyes, she felt a certain triumph at how far she'd come, and with it, the bittersweet awareness of lessons learned late.

She was smiling at her own sentimentality and struggling out of bed when the calico cat darted past her feet. "You again? Where did you come from?"

Watching it slip under the armoire and disappear, she noticed for the first time that the wardrobe wasn't flush against the wall. Curious, she grabbed her robe from the back of the chair, slipped it on and went over to investigate.

"Dear God," she breathed, backing away, staring at the open passageway door. Her first impulse was to call the management, but the possibility that this had something to do with Justin's disappearance made her hesitate. The wiser move might be to check it out herself first.

Even with the light streaming in from the bedroom, the musty stairway Lauren explored was dark and nearly unnavigable. She took one step a time, shuddering at the cobwebs that clung to her and calling softly for the cat. It occurred to her that the stairway probably led to the dungeon where Sam Lord kept Lucy. Hearing the crackle of rotted wood beneath her feet, she hesitated on the landing to the second flight of stairs. In the dim light, she could just make out the bottom. It looked like a tunnel with several passageways branching out in different directions, but there was no sign of Justin—or the cat.

A sound from above startled her. At first she thought it was a cat's cry. Listening again, she realized it was the telephone in her room. She turned and rushed up the stairway, bursting into the room just as the phone went silent.

Breathing heavily, sinking onto the bed, she stared at the phone. And suddenly it rang again, two short blasts that startled her heart into a cartwheel. *Let it be him,* she thought, hesitating a second before she picked it up.

"Hello?"

The line was silent, so silent Lauren could hear her own blood squeaking through her veins, and yet she knew someone was there. She could hear labored breathing. "Hello? Who is it?"

The voice that answered was male, raspy and unfamiliar. "The man you were with last night? If you ever want to see him again, listen carefully."

"Justin?" Lauren's heart faltered. "Do you mean Justin?"

"Yes."

"If I want to see him again? What does that mean? *Where is he?*"

"He's in trouble, Ms. Cambridge, a lot of trouble."

"Oh God, is he all right? Has he been hurt?"

"I can't tell you any more over the phone."

"Who *is* this?" she asked.

Silence again. "My name is Jack Slater," he said finally, traces of a British accent in his gravelly voice. "I own The Scarab. I believe you know that establishment?"

"Yes, I know it."

"Good, Duncan will bring you out here. In fact, he's waiting for you at the castle entrance now. I'd suggest you don't keep him waiting too long."

The phone clicked in Lauren's ear. Shaken, she nearly dropped the receiver as she tried to hang it up. Justin in trouble? What could that mean? She sat, paralyzed a moment, and then she flew into action, stumbling into the bathroom to wash her face, hurrying to dress.

It was as she was bending to put on her sandals that she saw the folded note on the floor next to the dresser. She snatched it up, straining to decipher the scribbled words.

Lauren—another emergency.
I'll contact you. Don't leave the island until you hear from me.
Justin

The note was barely legible, as though it had been written in great haste. Fingering the paper, Lauren turned back and stared at the armoire, the passageway. What was going on? When had he written this note? Confused, she read the last line of the note again. She had no plans to leave the island until the end of her vacation, a week away. Justin knew that, so the line had to mean that he hadn't intended to come back right away. At least not when he'd written it. Had something happened to him since?

Her skin prickled with foreboding as she remembered Justin's warning to stay away from Slater, something about his fleecing tourists. He'd also warned her to stay away from Duncan, who was waiting for her downstairs. The idea of being chauffeured anywhere by Duncan, especially to The Scarab, was a frightening prospect under any circumstances, but she had to go. *If you ever want to see him again,* Slater had said.

Sick with fear, Lauren grabbed her purse and started for the door.

Ten

If the exterior of The Scarab inspired thoughts of cut-throats and corruption, the interior confirmed them. Lauren knew the minute she walked in the door that she'd penetrated the dark underbelly of the island. At ten in the morning the small, murky bar was thick with horseflies and whispering patrons huddled over half-filled bottles of liquor. There wasn't a window in the place, and just one naked light bulb dangled from the ceiling above the bar. Justin had called the bar a "den of thieves." Drawing in a tight breath, Lauren decided he'd seriously understated it.

A lizard shimmied up the dry-rotted wall to her right. She suppressed a shudder and looked around for someone in charge. Across the room, a heavyset, titian-haired woman finished serving mugs of beer to a group of sinister-looking types and waved at Lauren. "What'll it be, ducky? A drink?" she called out in her raspy Cockney accent. The woman approached Lauren laboriously, a curious smile on her face.

Lauren didn't return the smile. Niceties in a place like this would target her as an easy mark. This was a rough crowd, and if she didn't look like she belonged, at least she could talk like she belonged.

"Tell Jack Slater that Lauren Cambridge is here." She barely had the words out of her mouth before half the room had swung around to stare at her.

"Slater?" the barmaid guffawed. "You sure, ducks?"

"He's expecting me."

"Right then." The woman's shrug said it's your funeral, lady. "I'll tell 'im your here." She zigzagged a diagonal path around the tables and disappeared through a beaded doorway.

Lauren edged next to a battle-scarred, "out of order" cigarette machine to wait, her mind on Slater's menacing message. By the looks of this place, if Justin really *was* in trouble, she was going to need some help. Duncan was parked out front, but she couldn't count on him for anything. She'd be lucky if he even stuck around long enough to drive her back. Her thoughts were abruptly cut off as a lizard skittered across the floor in front of her. Lauren stared at it without flinching, aware that she was still under scrutiny. Stay cool, she told herself, these hoodlums are like animals, they can smell fear.

Several things occurred to her as she waited. She

should have called Justin's bungalow before she left—
and stopped at the desk to see if he'd checked out. God,
yes, she ought to have done some investigating on her
own before leaping into Duncan's cab. But Slater hadn't
given her the chance. He'd made it sound like life or
death.

"'Ey, miss," the barmaid called, waving at her from
the doorway. "Come on back. Mr. Slater'll see you
now."

Jack Slater was undoubtedly one of the largest and
most unpleasant-looking people that Lauren had ever
seen. A great, hulking gorilla of a man with coppery red
hair and a full beard, he was sprawled gracelessly on a
tiny, creaking steno chair behind a rusting metal desk.
The room, a small, closetlike office with a groaning
ceiling fan overhead and jagged cracks in the plaster-
board walls, seemed barely large enough to contain him.

He leaned back, scrutinizing Lauren as she pushed
through the beads and approached his desk.

"Mr. Slater?" she said. "I got here as fast as I could.
What's going on? Where is Justin?"

"Sit down and have a drink, Ms. Cambridge." He
poured a splash of whiskey into a grimy glass and held
it up to her.

Lauren declined both the drink and the chair with a
shake of her head. "You said there was trouble, that
Justin was in trouble."

Slater took his sweet time topping off the drink. After
a long, slow swallow, he cleared his throat. "Perhaps I
should have said he *will* be in trouble—when I find him."

"Find him?" Lauren stared at him incredulously. "But you said if I ever wanted to see him again. You implied that he was here, or that you knew where he was."

"Yes, I suppose I did imply that," he said, the British accent evident again. "Rather clever of me, wasn't it?"

"My God, it was a trick? Why?" Even before she'd said the words, Lauren knew the answer. He'd lied to get her out here. Her heart hammering, she glanced behind her and saw the one-eyed man hovering outside the office door. "What's going on, Slater?" she snapped, covering fear with indignation. "What do you want with me? And where is Justin Dunne?"

Slater's lips curled back in a grin. "Is that what he's calling himself now? Justin Dunne?"

"Calling himself *now*? What's that supposed to mean?"

The huge man drank down the whiskey and slammed the glass on the desk, fracturing it with several hairline cracks. Heedlessly, he filled the glass again. "You made a mistake, Ms. Cambridge. You should have talked to me the other day when Duncan drove you out here. We could have saved each other a great deal of grief."

Lauren wouldn't be diverted. "What are you saying? That his name *isn't* Justin Dunne?"

Slater gleamed at her through pale blue eyes, incongruously tiny for the size of his head. "His legal name is Justin Coulter. Dunne was an alias, part of his cover."

Lauren's breathing went shallow. Instinctively she knew she didn't want to hear any more, that she was opening up a Pandora's box. "Cover?" she said thinly. "I don't understand."

"I think you had better sit down now, Ms. Cambridge," he suggested. "I have a great deal of information that may be of interest to you."

She shook her head as he waved to the chair behind her. "What information?"

He smiled malevolently, obviously enjoying himself. "Your friend, Justin Dunne, didn't come to Barbados on vacation as he may have told you," he said smugly. "Nor did he sail in from Trinidad. That sloop docked in Bridgetown, *The Witch Doctor*? It doesn't belong to him, Ms. Cambridge. It's a charter." He rolled back in the chair again and wiped a dribble of whiskey from his beard with the back of his hand. "He's lied to you—about everything."

Lauren took a measured breath and tried to control the creeping sense of dread in the pit of her stomach. "Why would he do that?" she asked cautiously. "And where is he now?"

"He got away from my men, and escaped the island last night—on a private plane—chartered, I assume. I don't know his destination. If I did—"

"Escaped? Why? What has he done?"

"He stole a ring that belongs to me, an antique ring, irreplaceable, of course, worth a fortune." He took another healthy slug of the liquor. "Whatever he may have told you, Ms. Cambridge, Coulter is a dangerous man."

Lauren didn't respond. Her mind was racing, and

even though sanity told her not to believe Slater, the dread in her stomach had become a sickening ripple of fear.

"He calls himself a treasure hunter, and, in fact, the ring he stole is over a hundred and fifty years old. They say it was part of Sam Lord's take from one of the English frigates he lured up onto the reefs. I don't know how Lord got the ring, and I don't care. He made a gift of it to my great, great grandfather, and that makes the ring mine. Unfortunately, it was stolen from my ancestor, and it's been lost ever since—until Coulter found it, that is."

"Found it? But you said he stole it. Perhaps he didn't know it was yours."

Slater's pasty complexion reddened. "He knew. The police threw him off the island six months ago for breaking and entering. He was ransacking this office. His intention all along has been to steal the ring. Perhaps you didn't know that the ring's value goes beyond the material, Ms. Cambridge. The islanders are terrified of its magic, so, of course, the man who possesses it wields great power." The chair creaked as he sat forward. "Think about it. Would an honest man go to such lengths—the secrecy, the elaborate cover? And why else would he involve you?"

"Me?"

"You very conveniently had a room at Sam Lord's—" his mouth tightened in a smile "—which is where the ring's been hidden all these years as it turns out. And how handy for Coulter. An assignation with a beautiful woman? What better way to get access to the castle in the small hours of the morning. And if the theft should be discovered and reported, or if any other irregularities should occur, the room is registered in your name, not his."

Lauren's throat constricted painfully. "How do I know that any of this is true?"

"It's *all* true. Check it out. And check with the local police while you're at it. They've got a file on him."

Searching for some way to refute him, Lauren grasped at straws. "If you knew he was on the island searching for the ring, why didn't you notify the police?"

"Use your head, Ms. Cambridge. I wanted him to lead me to the ring first."

A lizard darted up the wall behind Slater. Watching it halt and twitch its tail, Lauren was gripped with nausea. The bitter, metallic taste of fear and disgust foamed in her throat. I've got to get out of this place, she thought, stepping back, whirling to leave.

Slater lurched up from his desk. "Nothing's for free, Ms. Cambridge. I gave you information. Now you owe me some. Where has Coulter gone?"

Lauren swung back, startled. "I don't know where he's gone, Mr. Slater. If I did, I wouldn't be here."

"I hope you can convince me of that."

A nerve jumped near Lauren's eye. "Are you threatening me, Slater?" Gathering her wits, she glanced at her watch. "Do you think I'm a fool? I told people I was coming out here, and if I'm not back within the hour, this place will be swarming with police."

Pressing his massive fists to the desk, Slater leaned forward and stared at her for what seemed like a lifetime. "Get out of my bar," he said, grinding the words into a low snarl. "Tell Coulter I'll find him, and when I do, he'll wish he'd never heard of me."

"I wish I'd never heard of you."

Lauren sent the beads swinging on her way out. Frightened and angry, she stormed past the grinning one-eyed man and banged out of the bar.

Duncan was hovering near the Rover, wide-eyed with concern. "You okay?" he asked, rushing up to her.

"That man is scum, Duncan," she said, brushing by him. "How could you work for him?"

"I don't work him," he insisted, hurrying to catch up with her. Lauren halted to look at him.

Duncan shrugged. "He pay me bring you here. I bring you here. He pay me leave message. I leave message."

"Message?" Lauren stared at him. Remembering the note the hotel clerk had given her the night of the garden party, she began to put it all together. "So that's what you were doing at the party. You were supposed to bring me out here, to The Scarab?"

Duncan's eyes were large and guileless. "I be working man," he said. "I got wife, three hungry kids."

Lauren nodded, distracted by a flash of fear. Had Slater been trying to warn her all along, secretly, without alerting Justin? And did that mean that some—or all— of what he said about Justin was true? The fear curled in her stomach, chilling her. She dreaded the answers to those questions, but she would never have any peace until she knew. "Duncan, there are places I need to go, people I need to talk to. Will you take me? Will you help me?"

He nodded so quickly Lauren wondered if she could trust him. His rationale about working for Slater was a little too opportunistic to suit her, but she was reasonably sure he felt no special allegiance for the man. She would need transportation, and a local like Duncan, who knew the island, would be invaluable to her in checking out Slater's information.

"Let's go," Duncan said, grinning. "You pay, I drive."

Lauren shook her head. "I've got a better idea. I'll pay and *I'll* drive."

Lauren managed pretty well driving the Rover, despite the fact that the gearshift came off in her hand twice and Duncan insisted on stopping to pick up fares. The distractions took her mind off Justin temporarily, but they couldn't stem the tide of impending doom she felt. Justin's mysterious nature, the things he'd told her, the things he'd kept from her, gave Slater's story a ring of truth. By the time they reached Bridgetown, Lauren felt a desperate need to know if Justin had lied to her, and a deep, abiding fear that he had.

The first blow came in Bridgetown at Island Yachts, where she learned that Slater had been right about the sloop. *The Witch Doctor* was an island charter. It had arrived from Martinque two days before she met Justin.

The Bajan woman at the small yacht brokerage declined to tell Lauren who'd chartered it, but when Duncan intervened, alternately pleading and berating the woman, she opened a book and pointed to the name Justin Dunne.

A half hour later, exiting the police department, Lauren held out the faint hope that her premonition might be wrong. She'd learned that Justin Coulter, an American citizen, had been questioned on suspicion of breaking and entering six months before, released for lack of evidence, and warned to leave the island. Coulter's physical description was frighteningly similar to Justin Dunne, except that Coulter was smaller in stature and had no mustache. It was a straw—the proverbial straw—but Lauren clung to it, praying that Dunne and Coulter weren't the same man.

Her fragile optimism increased by the time she reached Sam Lord's. She questioned the registration clerk with the taut obsessiveness of a woman who knew the answers might bring her pain.

"We have no Justin Coulter registered," the clerk said politely.

"What about a Justin Dunne?" Lauren asked. The clerk checked and nodded. "In Bungalow 10?" Lauren pressed.

"Yes, but he checked out early this morning."

"Did he say where he was going?"

The woman shook her head. Lauren thanked her, wondering what to do next. Justin Dunne had checked out, but she still didn't know if he and Coulter were the same man.

"Did you say Coulter?" a man asked.

Lauren's head snapped up. It was the same night clerk who'd helped her with the feral cat. He was emerging from an interior office, carrying a stack of visitor's guides.

"Yes," Lauren clipped the word off in her nervousness. "Why?"

The clerk approached the counter. "We got a telegram the other day for a Justin Coulter. The guy in Bungalow 10 claimed it." He shrugged and set the guides down on the counter. "I'm still not sure we did the right thing, giving it to him. Do you happen to know the guy?"

She shook her head, her heart thudding painfully. "No. I thought I did…but I guess not." Turning away from the counter and the man, she walked through the lobby to the front entrance. A laughing couple burst through the doors, jostling her rudely. "Excuse me," she murmured, barely aware of them, or of the pain that shot through her shoulder. Outside, Duncan was still waiting at the bottom of the steps with the Rover.

"Where to next?" he asked as she approached him.

Her throat tightened. "I guess this is it, Duncan. The end of the line." Drawing in a long breath, she willed herself not to become emotional. Dunne and Coulter were the same man, that seemed fairly obvious. She was too muddled to know what that meant at the moment except that her hopes had been thrown back in her face, and her heart felt tender and hot in her chest.

"You find him?" Duncan asked, concern in his voice.

"No, not exactly." Staring at his sober face, Lauren found it impossible to say anything else. She dug into the pocket of her slacks and came out with some cash, several Barbadian bills she'd tucked in there. "Here," she said, poking the money into his hand. "I hope it's enough."

He nodded and gave her a lopsided smile. "You be some good driver," he said.

"Good driver?"

He patted the door of the Rover, and Lauren recognized by his quick nod that he was trying to cheer her up. She felt her throat welling with sadness. "Oh, Duncan, thank you. And thank you for helping me, too. You be some good driver yourself."

He beamed at her, and when she tried to smile back, her mouth trembled with the awkwardness of it, bringing her own distress into sharp focus. "Thanks again," she said, then hurried up the stairs, not stopping until she got to her room.

Hours later she was sitting in the darkened room by the window, the note in her lap, dazed, wondering about the man who'd written it. She knew his name, Justin Coulter. But who was he? Had he done the things Slater accused him of? Had he used her to get to the ring? She was sure only of the answer to the last question. Yes, he'd used her. The ring was the personal mission he'd referred to, and she was the pawn, the instrument of his ambition, obsession, or whatever it was that drove him.

She rose from the chair and turned on the light, wincing as it illuminated the room. Looking around at the canopied bed, the armoire, she thought about what had happened in this room the night before—the passion, the tenderness, the miracles—and her heart tightened with angry pain. How could he? She stared at the bed, remembering. "You bastard," she whispered, shaking her head. "Was it all strategy? The rescues, the sightseeing, the Castle Dinner?" Her heart twisted. "Even the lovemaking?"

The white dress she'd worn lay over the back of the chair. She strode across the room, scooped it up and stared at the wrinkled chiffon, remembering how he'd touched her. *"Oh God,"* she moaned, flinging the dress down. Her voice cracked, and the tears began to stream. She slumped into the chair, fighting against the ache in her throat, the brutal intensity of her feelings. She was breaking apart inside.

A sob ripped at her control. Rocking with the pain, she cried for all the years of denial, for love torn away like a kidnapped child. And finally, as the tears subsided, she closed her eyes and lay her head back. Her temples throbbed with an incipient headache. Her chest was tight, and her heart felt fragile and torn, like tissue paper. She couldn't remember ever feeling so bruised and buffeted before, not since her childhood when her father left that last time and never came back. Her mother's words had been so bitter. "He's cruel and selfish, your father. He doesn't care who he hurts."

My mother must have loved him very much, Lauren realized, to hate him so much. She supposed that was what happened to women who were used and discarded. They grew bitter like her mother, hating men the rest of their lives, hating everything that stirred love in them, because love meant pain.

Memories flooded her, past mixing with present until she couldn't distinguish the old heartache from the new. And finally, exhausted, she fell asleep, sitting in the chair, her hands curled at her chest. With dawn just two or three hours away, she slept fitfully, in limbo between the waking world and her troubled dreams. When the phone rang at eight, she woke with a start, her heart rocketing.

"Hello?" she said, her voice a raspy whisper.

"Lauren? It's me, Rene. Are you okay?"

Rene? Lauren clutched the receiver with both hands and rocked forward. She'd thought it would be him. *It was supposed to be him.*

"Lauren, are you there? I'm sorry if I woke you, kiddo. It's later here, and I'm just dying to hear what's going on. Lauren?"

"I'm here," she said, her head throbbing, her heart in a vise.

"Are you all right? Lauren what's wrong?"

"Nothing's wrong." Lauren knew she couldn't talk about what had happened yet, not without bringing back that terrible feeling of breaking apart. Looking around the room, she realized she couldn't stay here any longer. Everything would remind her of him, even the sunlight pouring through the window. If she stayed, she would wait for the phone to ring, pray for the phone to ring. No, she couldn't go through that.

Staring down at the dress on the floor, she was

numbly aware of Rene demanding to know what was wrong. "Nothing's wrong, Rene," she said finally. "I'm coming home, that's all."

She packed slowly, her senses alert for any sound, a knock at the door, a ring of the telephone. Foolishly, she looked for him at every turn as she left, in the lobby of the castle, when she got into Duncan's cab for the trip to the airport, when she boarded the plane. Finally, as the plane's wheels left the runway, and they soared into the air, she knew it was over.

Eleven

Lauren sat at a window table in the small, elegant Cantonese restaurant, Rene's favorite lunch spot, and waited for her friend to arrive. Outside on the street, the business lunch crowd had thinned, and pale sunlight filtered through the overcast to sheen the rain-slicked streets.

Lauren sipped plum wine and gazed out at the sights, traces of sadness, resignation and relief in her expression. She was back in Seattle. She was home.

Touching the fanlike folds of a white linen napkin, artfully arranged in her crystal water goblet, she thought how different this restaurant was from the casual, open-air style in Barbados. No scented trade winds here, no birds flitting down to land on your table while you ate. But, then, perhaps any business-district bistro would compare unfavorably to the languid flow of life in the tropics.

She'd been back a week, actually, but only now that she'd returned to work and acclimated to the brisk weather and the even brisker pace of her fifteen-hour workdays, did she feel like she'd really returned. Probably, she thought, a part of her would never return. She still hurt inside, the kind of hurting that felt like emptiness where joy and anticipation had been.

"Lauren?"

Her head snapped up as Rene bounced up to her, lifted her out of the chair and hugged her enthusiastically.

"Oh, Rene, how are you?" Lauren said, her eyes misting as she hugged her friend back.

They broke from the embrace and looked at each other, smiling, laughing as though it had been forever. "I'm fine," Rene assured her. "The question is how are *you*? Why haven't you called? Why didn't you return my messages?"

Rene signaled the waiter for a glass of wine as they sat.

"I did call," Lauren reminded her, "the day I got back. I told you everything, every excruciating detail. Don't you remember that marathon session in your office? I cried. *We cried.* I swore off men forever?"

Rene laughed and shrugged out of her raincoat. "Of course I remember that. How could I forget your plan to flood the water supply with a virus that targeted the Y chromosome? But it's been a week since then, and I haven't heard a peep out of you. How are you doing?"

"I'm fine." Lauren laughed, a little wistfully. "Look at me. I'm here, aren't I?" Her expression softened, saddened. "Yeah, all right, it still hurts. It hurts like crazy, but I'm muddling through. And I'm going to be okay."

Rene took her hand, squeezed it. "I know you are," she said softly and paused for a moment. "Just holler if I'm getting too nosy, but where've you been this last week? What have you been doing?"

"Working. Thinking."

"Uh-oh. Is the male population safe?"

"Oh, I suppose." Lauren sighed in mock regret and winked at her friend. "I've worked through the retribution fantasies, but it's kind of ironic, don't you think, that the first man I met in my quest to discover the romantic side of Lauren Cambridge was a scoundrel. A devastatingly sexy, *sensitive* scoundrel." Her voice caught slightly. "I could be very bitter about that if I'd let myself."

"But you won't let yourself?"

Lauren shook her head and smiled over the sudden lump in her throat. "I'm not going to be like her, Rene," she said, rubbing her thumb along the delicate stem of the wineglass. "I'm not going to end up like my mother."

Rene pursed her lips. "Good."

"I've had a week to think about how it feels to be used, to be abandoned, and I understand my mother's pain. *God*, I've been living her pain, and it hurts...but I think I've learned something from it."

Rene smiled, affection sparkling in her eyes.

"Justin didn't take anything away from me," Lauren said, "not really. He gave me something."

"How's that?"

"He gave me tears and joy and ecstasy. He gave me the combination to the safe I've been hoarding my emotions in." Tears misted her eyes. "I feel things now, Rene, so intensely that I can't back away from them. I'm swamped with love and hurt and indignation."

"Love?"

Lauren smiled, sighed. "Yeah, that's the hard part, that's the hell of it really."

"You fell in love with him?"

Looking down, Lauren entwined her fingers. Finally she nodded.

Rene reached over and touched her hand. "Oh, Lauren...I'm sorry."

"Don't be." She shrugged, braver than she felt. "'Tis better to have loved and lost."

"Than never to have loved at all," Rene finished the quote for her. "I guess you're right."

They were both quiet for a time, Lauren gazing into the amber depths of her wineglass, Rene staring out the window. Lauren spoke first.

"He left me a note, you know, said he was coming back. I'll always wonder what would have happened if I'd stayed."

"Lauren," Rene said gently, "you did the best thing under the circumstances. Even if he *had* returned, what would you have done then? The man lied to you; he stole a valuable ring. That's no way to start a relationship."

Lauren nodded.

"You have to move on," Rene continued, "take what you've learned and move on. Listen," she said, patting Lauren's hand, smiling, "do you remember Plan A?"

"Plan A?"

"Yeah, that wild and crazy guy, that friend of Ted's I told you about before you went on vacation? I know you don't want to rush into anything, but he's apparently back in town, and if you'd like to— Lauren, don't look at me like that, stop shaking your head. Lauren, put down that *wineglass*!"

Lauren left Cambridge Investments late that night, exhausted as always, but with the satisfaction of having doubled an elderly retiree's investment income and landed a big corporate account, among her many other transactions. It felt like a good day's work.

The short trip to her apartment in Lake Forest Park went quickly in the light, late evening traffic. Wondering if she had any salad makings in the refrigerator, she let herself into her two-bedroom town house and switched on the lights. The familiar French country decor and profusion of houseplants greeted her, but something was amiss. Her blue-point Siamese cat wasn't curled up on the window seat.

"Burger King?" she called, and then whistled, expecting him to bound into the room like the attack dog he seemed to think he was. She dropped her raincoat on the sofa and called again. This time an anxious meow answered her. It came from her bedroom off the hallway. Odd, she thought, heading for her room, that plaintive cry didn't sound anything like Burger King's usual robust yowl. "Kitty?" she called again.

Entering the room, she saw the cat on her bed, pacing nervously, his ears pricked.

"*There* you are." She stroked and hugged him in her relief, then sat beside him, bending to pull off her high heels. The cat mewed again, urgently, bumping against her. "What's wrong with you, fella?" she crooned. "Did you miss me?"

In what had become a ritual in three years of living with a Siamese that demanded lots of attention, Lauren rubbed his chin with one hand while attempting to undress with the other. She had her skirt off and was undoing her blouse when Burger King mewed again. The sound of it made Lauren's skin prickle. Something was wrong.

Suddenly a shadow fell across the bed. Lauren froze, and then she whirled, her heart beating so hard she couldn't speak. Justin stood in the doorway, spectrally backlit by the glow from the living room lights. The outline of his body loomed huge and surreal, a magnificent apparition.

"Why don't you ask me if *I* missed you?" he asked.

Lauren staggered backward in her shock. "*Justin?* How—"

"How did I find you? It wasn't easy."

He moved out of the doorway, and even in the dim

light, Lauren could see the icy luminescence of his eyes. Poised between light and shadow, he looked wild and beautiful to her stunned senses.

"How *did* you find me? What are you doing here?" she asked.

"I had no choice."

The words were exhaled more than spoken, and Lauren was riveted by the exhaustion and trapped fury in his voice.

"Now answer *my* question," he said. "Why the hell didn't you wait for me?"

"Justin, I—"

She gasped as he closed the distance between them and caught her by the arm. "I don't think I'd ever known what panic was," he breathed, "until I got back to that island and found you'd gone. I went after Duncan first, scared him half to death. He told me you'd talked to Slater, but before I could get to Slater, somebody warned him." He hesitated, his grip on her arm tightening. "I finally caught up with the SOB in Jamaica, and we settled our differences. I know what he told you, Lauren. What I don't understand is why you believed him."

Lauren's throat was so dry she could barely talk. "What was I supposed to believe? He said you stole a priceless ring, he said you used me to find it, he said—"

"Listen to me. That ring belongs to my grandmother. It was willed to her by her grandfather, John Coulter, a British trader who was lost in a shipwreck on Cobbler's Reef. The ship was looted and the ring stolen—by Sam Lord, according to a ship's journal that was salvaged."

"The ring was yours?"

"My family's, yes. The ring had an interlocking part, a gold band, with John Coulter's name engraved on the shank. The band was found, returned to Coulter's widow and eventually passed down to my grandmother. The stolen half was a water sapphire set in eighteen-karat gold."

"Water sapphire?" Lauren remembered his remark about her eyes the day they met. "Why didn't you tell me about the ring? Why didn't you tell me what was going on?"

He released her, shaking his head. "Slater wanted the ring, too, and I'd involved you enough without endangering you with information he was desperate for."

Rubbing her arm where he'd held her, Lauren listened, transfixed, as he described an island myth about an ancestor of Slater's who'd stolen the ring from Sam Lord and died a macabre death. He recounted the islanders' belief that the ring held the power of love and death, and then, pacing the room, he told her about a Bajan woman mentioned in his grandmother's journals who'd been married to Slater's ancestor. She'd hidden the ring in the castle after his death, thinking it would lift the curse. "She had a descendant on the island," he said, turning to Lauren, "a bizarre old woman mixed up with voodoo." He went on, explaining how he'd tried to find the woman on an earlier trip to Barbados, and how he'd been framed and thrown off the island on trumped-up charges brought by Slater. And finally he came to his meeting with Lauren.

"I guess some people would think it was purely by accident that my jeep broke down that morning, and that you happened to be in that taxi I flagged down." From across the room, he searched her features as though he were seeking answers to life's mysteries. "I don't know anymore, Lauren. I'm beginning to wonder if anything's accidental. I'm even beginning to wonder if the myth about the ring is true. The Bajans believe the ring's interconnecting halves were lovers. Torn apart, its power became destructive."

Lauren's silence came of simple incredulity. She was unable to absorb it all.

"I'm sorry I had to mix you up in this," he said, "but I'd run out of options. I had one shot at finding that Bajan woman, and the clock was running."

"The clock was running? What do you mean?"

He went quiet and turned away, massaging his neck. "My grandmother was ill, gravely ill. She wanted to see the ring intact and back in the family where it belonged while she was still alive."

"Oh, Justin, I'm sorry."

His jaw flexed against some emotion he wasn't ready to acknowledge. "She suffers from congestive heart failure," he said quietly. "She's still critical, but she made it through the last crisis, and the doctors are hopeful."

"And you were able to give her the ring?"

"Yes, thank God. I think if anything helped bring her through, it was that. Recovering the sapphire has been an obsession of hers since she found the journals a few years ago."

His shoulders rose and fell with a slow, deliberate breath. Lauren could see the trapped emotion in his features, and it pulled at something deep within her. It also dawned on her slowly, incredulously, that he may have risked his life to find her. He'd chased Slater all over the Caribbean, tracked her down here, to Seattle, to this apartment. "Justin, why did you come here?"

His expression transformed as he looked at her, a gradual intensity that built in his eyes like a darkening flame. "I told you before—I didn't have any choice. When I got back to the island you were gone." His voice roughened. "I *had* to find you."

The undercurrents in his statement made Lauren's throat go dry. She instinctively brought her hand to her breast and touched her own bare skin, startling herself as she remembered she was wearing only a half-buttoned blouse and her slip.

He noticed it, too, as though for the first time. His eyes flashed over her body, sweeping her with their heat. His gaze stopped at her breasts, at her open blouse, and Lauren could almost see the desire flare through him. His whole body tautened.

Reacting from some female instinct she barely understood, Lauren reached down, her heart pounding, her fingers shaking, and began to undo the rest of her blouse. She knew by the quick, violent word he exhaled that she was arousing him, and God, some crazy part of her wanted that. She wanted to drive him wild. She wanted him so tight with desire, he was shaking, bursting.

"Lauren—"

"No—" She raised her hand, holding him at bay with the urgency in her voice. "No, please Justin, you asked me to do this once before, and I couldn't. Now I can, *I want to.*"

With every button she worked open, Lauren felt a tiny, exquisite curling sensation deep inside her. In the next seconds her nerves, her muscles, went rigid with riveting excitement. And by the time she freed the last button and let the blouse slide off her shoulders, she was the one who was tight with desire. *She* was shaking, bursting.

Staring into Justin's eyes, her heart pounding wildly, she drew the slip straps off her shoulders. She wore no bra and the silk floating over her skin was mesmerizing. *The wildfire in his eyes was mesmerizing.*

"Lauren," he warned, *"finish it.* If you don't take that slip off, I will."

The slip dropped to the floor, and Lauren gasped as Justin enveloped her like a breaking storm. He swept her into his arms, lifting her off the floor, thrilling her, drowning her senses with his urgent, bruising passion. His mouth was a fire storm; his arms were a buffeting force of nature.

The next seconds were a blur of unbridled passion as he ripped off his clothes and they fell on the bed together, rolling to their sides, all urgent thrusting limbs and wild need. Lauren moaned in her throat as Justin lifted her leg and drove into her deeply and swiftly. He was golden and savage, proud and possessed, and his thrusts were the sweetest, purest pleasure she'd ever known. Her body was an exquisitely receptive musical instrument, resonating to his every touch, his every kiss, responding with the most beautiful melodies she'd ever heard…sighs and cries and the spiraling bells of ecstasy. Their coupling was so abandoned, so intense, that it was only seconds before she was soaring and spiraling, bursting like a star shower, lost in the glory of it all.

The tears came spontaneously, flowing from some painful place in Lauren's heart that had never known this kind of joy. "Oh, Justin," she said, unable to stop herself, "I love you." Tangling her fingers in his hair, entwining his body with her legs, she clung to him, achingly vulnerable. She loved him, *God, she loved him….*

She peaked again and again, but the ultimate moment of surrender was a beautiful, harrowing thing that melted her body and drenched her senses. It was rocketing joy and naked need.

For Justin, surrender came with the thundering flight of his heart, the excruciating pressure in his loins. Her body caressed him like a mystical force, and his control ebbed with every shudder that went through her. Finally, with a low, savage moan, he lost the battle to a shock wave that shook him, body and soul. It was violent and luminous, an exploding wall of white. He'd never felt such delirious power before. He'd never felt such a draining, cleansing weakness.

For some time afterward, they lay together, mesmerized by the drifting, lingering rapture. Lauren gazed up at him, caught by the melting tenderness in his eyes.

"Do you always cry?" he asked, brushing her tears away with his thumb.

"No, never before," she said softly. "Not until you."

He exhaled as though someone had hit him in the stomach. "God, I love you," he said, the words tumbling out, uncontrolled and unplanned.

For a split second Lauren couldn't breathe.

He must have seen the disbelief in her eyes. "I do love you," he said, gathering her up, a fierceness in his arms, in his voice. He held her so tightly she moaned with the sharp pleasure of it. "Am I hurting you?" he asked, releasing her, cradling her face with his hands. "God, I'm sorry. I can't help myself with you. Nobody and nothing in my life had ever made me feel the way you do." He hesitated, his blue eyes penetrating her like a laser. "I've got a confession for you. Are you ready for this?"

"Oh no, please," she mumbled, half-serious in her apprehension. "What is it? You're married? A priest? An escaped felon?"

"A priest?" He grimaced in mock despair and pulled her into his arms. "Come here, you little idiot, I need to tell you this. I've never bared my soul to anyone, so this is a first."

She snuggled into him rapturously, resting her head on his shoulder. "In that case, I'm honored. Confess away."

He was quiet a moment, and Lauren waited patiently, letting herself be rocked by his steady breathing. His voice sounded faraway when he finally spoke.

"They say some men are born with the wanderlust," he said, stroking her hair absently. "I always figured I was one of them. I guess I've been searching all my life, hungry for something that eluded me. My work is a challenge, and the treasure hunting gave me temporary satisfaction—diving off the Florida Keys for sunken treasure, sluicing for gold at Sutter's Mill—but it was never enough. There was always something more that I wanted—or needed—only I didn't know what it was."

She waited for him to go on, and when he didn't, she crooked her head to look up at him. "A safe harbor?" she suggested softly. "Or the love of a good woman?"

He smiled down at her, traces of sadness vanishing as he bent to kiss her nose. "Now that you mention it, yes, I guess that's exactly what it was."

"Which?"

"Both." Passion raked through his voice as he shifted to his side and pulled her to him. "I didn't sleep for a week trying to find you. I'm not even sure I ate. I've never been so obsessed in my life." He stared into her eyes as though seeing something that drew him in and captured him. When he kissed her, it was with thrilling restraint, brushing his lips over hers, cherishing her mouth as though it was a delicate thing that might break with too rough handling. "I belong with you, Lauren," he said, reaching down to press his palm to her naked belly. His voice was textured with husky desire. "And I belong here, inside you."

Lauren felt it instantly, the kindling flare of sexual longing, and she automatically tensed to stop it. It astonished her how susceptible she was to this man—a touch, a look, and she was reduced to quivering need. He wanted to make love to her again, and this time it would be gentle and slow and unbearably tender, she knew that, she could see it in his eyes. But she couldn't let that happen, not now. She caught hold of his hand, clasped it firmly. "Justin, please, you just said you *belong* with me. I have to know what that means."

"It means now that I've found you, I'm not letting you out of my sight again. It means I'm going to stay close at hand—as close as you'll let me." Grinning faintly, he lifted her hand to his mouth and pressed his lips to it. "Here's to a safe harbor and the love of a good woman."

She laughed softly, joyously. "This good woman was hoping you'd say that." Ever practical, the next thoughts that entered Lauren's mind were of living arrangements and business matters. Inviting him to move in with her seemed a little bold at the moment, so she brought up the less sensitive issue. "What about your work, Justin? Don't you have an office somewhere? Aren't there arrangements to be made?"

He kissed the last knuckle of her little finger, and she felt the soft, blond hairs of his mustache gently abrade her skin. That was him, she thought, gentle and rough, both qualities so vividly drawn—and so unusual in one man.

"No, there's no office to close down," he told her. "I've been living and working out of hotel rooms, going wherever the job takes me for longer than I care to remember. Now that I think about it, I may open an office here." His eyes touched hers briefly as he placed a kiss in the vulnerable hollow of her palm. "Beyond that, it's just a question of getting in touch with some business contacts in this area. Matter of fact, I've got a meeting scheduled with a contractor friend of mine tomorrow, Ted Browning."

"Ted Browning?" Lauren rose up on her elbow to look at him. "Really? I know Ted."

By then Justin was too busy nibbling on her fingertips to pay much attention. "Is that right?" he murmured. "Ted and I went to school together back on the East Coast."

A nebulous connection was forming in Lauren's mind. "And Rene? Do you know his wife, Rene?"

He shrugged. "Not really. I met her once at a cocktail party a year or so ago. A psychiatrist, isn't she? I remember her checking me out and giving me one of those have-I-got-a-girl-for-you lines."

Lauren flashed back on the session with Rene before she'd left for Barbados. Rene had mentioned a man, a friend of Ted's, and when Lauren had objected strenuously, Rene had backed off with the remark about his being too wild and crazy for Lauren anyway. Today at lunch Rene had brought it up again. *Plan A, remember?* she'd said. *That friend of Ted's…apparently he's back in town.*

Justin's brows furrowed. "What? Have I got spinach on my teeth? Why are you staring at me like that?"

"Oh, my God! Justin…you're Plan A!"

* * *

The sensation of something moist and whiskery stroking her chin stirred Lauren from the depths of a deep sleep. "Justin?" she murmured, aware of a heavy weight oppressing her chest. She smiled, still too drowsy to open her eyes. Such a deliciously hairy man. She'd have to remind him to trim his mustache.

A rumbling sound startled her fully awake. Opening her eyes, she stared into the placid blue gaze of her cat. He was lying on her chest and purring like a lawn mower. She acknowledged the cat with a sleepy smile. "Morning, fella. I thought you were somebody else."

The cat began grooming himself lazily, indifferent to Lauren's attempt to move out from under him. "You're going on a diet," she threatened, imagining the newspaper headline: Woman Found Pinned To Bed By Huge Cat.

"Here we go," she said, clutching him and rolling to her side. Indignant, Burger King bounded out of her grasp, and Lauren sat up, straightening her nightgown and brushing herself off. It took her all of one microsecond to realize that the other side of the bed was empty. Justin was gone.

Her reaction was pure, reflexive panic. She looked around the room and found not a trace of him. Oh, no, she thought, oh God, *not again*. She knew it was ridiculous. He was probably in the kitchen, but she'd been abandoned one too many times to be rational. *"Justin?"*

The house was silent except for Burger King's routine grooming noises. Lauren struggled out of bed, darted for the living room and found it empty. She went through the rest of the condo, room by room, her heart beating rapidly. There was no sign of him anywhere, no sign that he'd ever been there. Dear God, she thought, standing in the living room and staring out the window at the misty rain, this was just the way he'd disappeared in Barbados.

It wasn't until she returned to her bedroom and sank onto the bed that she saw it. The corner of a folded note was nestled under the coverlet she'd thrown off. Lauren sprang up, staring at it, almost afraid to read it. As she tweaked it out from under the blanket, a ring fell out, it's smoky, blue-gray stone and intricate setting breathtakingly beautiful. Lauren scooped the ring up in her palm, mesmerized. She could see the interlocking parts, two spun gold bands woven like latticework around the brilliantly faceted sapphire. Opening the note with trembling fingers, she read a message that brought tears to her eyes and a sweet, stinging pain to the back of her throat.

Lauren, my grandmother wanted me to have the ring with her blessings, and her express wish was that I give it to a woman I could love and cherish forever. Please accept it as my promise that I will always come back.

Justin

"Oh God, Justin, where *are* you?" she whispered, reading the note again. The words filled her with a longing so unbearably sharp she was afraid to let herself believe them. She clutched the ring in her hand, turning as the front door opened.

A moment later, he appeared in the doorway to her bedroom, newspapers under his arm, a bakery box and a bouquet of flowers in his hand. "I see you found the note," he said softly. "I was afraid you might wake up while I was gone."

"I did," she said, "...wake up."

His smile was tender and sexy and full of male pride of possession. "I knew you'd be beautiful in the morning."

The flush of love Lauren felt for him at that moment was unexpected and radiant. In its wake she experienced a poignant stab of joy. He hadn't left her. He'd come back, *and with flowers*. She tried to fight back the tears, tried to stop the tiny, exquisite tearing sensation deep in her heart, but it was no use. Crumpling onto the bed, her chin trembling, she gave in to the flood tide of emotion. As the heartaches of the past merged with the burgeoning joy of the present, hot tears rolled down her cheeks, and she covered her face with her hands.

"Lauren, what's wrong?"

All she could do was shake her head as he sat beside her and held her in his arms. "Nothing, *nothing*," she mumbled. "It's the ring, it's the note. The words, they're *so* beautiful."

He held her for several moments, stroking her hair. "I sure hope you're the type who cries when you're happy," he said, turning her tear-streaked face up, concern in his eyes.

Lauren felt a spasm of emotion in her throat. "Oh, Justin, Justin, one of these days I'll have to tell you about my crazy problems with life and love, and then you'll understand." She opened her hand and looked at the ring, a sob catching in her throat. "And then you'll understand how much this means to me."

Turning into him, she burrowed into the warm strength of his shoulder and convulsed with a final shuddering sob. Sighing and spent, she rested against him, breathing deeply, aware of his hands stroking her hair, his lips pressing tender kisses to her temple. His touch was healing, and as warmth and energy began to stir in her again, she roused a little and looked up at him.

"You okay?" he asked.

"I think so."

"Okay enough to talk about us? Because if you're not, it can wait."

She smiled, her mouth unsteady. "Talk."

He laughed and kissed her eyelids, tasting her tears and blotting them with his fingers. "The first time I saw you," he said, taking her face in his hands, "I wondered if the color of your eyes was an omen. Now I know it was, a good omen. The ring has been lost for one hundred and fifty years, and I found it because of you. I found it *for* you."

Lauren experienced a surge of anticipation as he opened her hand, took the ring and slipped it onto her finger. In that one shimmering second, everything was suspended, her heartbeat, her respiration. She looked down at the beautiful stone, magical lights dancing in its faceted surfaces, and felt a vibrancy warming her hand. Struck by the fiery luminescence it gave off, the uncanny energy, she found it impossible not to wonder if the ring did have powers, if it had influenced their destinies.

Justin's voice floated through her consciousness as though it came from another time. "Belong to me, Lauren," he said. "Wear my ring forever…marry me… forever."

She looked up at him, and the passion, the promise in his eyes, were riveting. The faint, spellbinding smile she loved shadowed his features. "Say yes," he said, tipping her chin up, nearing until his lips were breathtakingly close to hers. "After all, I am Plan A."

Lauren felt a hot, sweet thrill as he took possession of her lips, lightly, a flitting butterfly's caress. His arms enclosed her, and in that brilliant instant of awareness, she felt it all, the drives that had brought them together, the needs that would bind them together…the passion for attachment, the cry for belonging.

She felt it all…with him.

As the kiss began to deepen, she pressed her fingers to his jaw, pulling back long enough to answer him. The ring flashed a brilliant light as she whispered, "Yes."

* * * * *

Mediterranean Nights

Join the guests and crew of Alexandra's Dream, *the newest luxury ship to set sail on the romantic Mediterranean, as they experience the glamorous world of cruising.*

A new Harlequin continuity series begins in June 2007 with
FROM RUSSIA, WITH LOVE
by Ingrid Weaver

Marina Artamova books a cabin on the luxurious cruise ship Alexandra's Dream, *when she finds out that her orphaned nephew and his adoptive father are aboard. She's determined to be reunited with the boy…but the romantic ambience of the ship and her undeniable attraction to a man she considers her enemy are about to interfere with her quest!*

Turn the page for a sneak preview!

Piraeus, Greece

"THERE SHE IS, Stefan. *Alexandra's Dream.*" David Anderson squatted beside his new son and pointed at the dark blue hull that towered above the pier. The cruise ship was a majestic sight, twelve decks high and as long as a city block. A circle of silver and gold stars, the logo of the Liberty Cruise Line, gleamed from the swept-back smokestack. Like some legendary sea creature born for the water, the ship emanated power from every sleek curve—even at rest it held the promise of motion. "That's going to be our home for the next ten days."

The child beside him remained silent, his cheeks

working in and out as he sucked furiously on his thumb. Hair so blond it appeared white ruffled against his forehead in the harbor breeze. The baby-sweet scent unique to the very young mingled with the tang of the sea.

"Ship," David said. "Uh, *parakhod*."

From beneath his bangs, Stefan looked at the *Alexandra's Dream*. Although he didn't release his thumb, the corners of his mouth tightened with the beginning of a smile.

David grinned. That was Stefan's first smile this afternoon, one of only two since they had left the orphanage yesterday. It was probably because of the boat—according to the orphanage staff, the boy loved boats, which was the main reason David had decided to book this cruise. Then again, there was a strong possibility the smile could have been a reaction to David's attempt at pocket-dictionary Russian. Whatever the cause, it was a good start.

The liaison from the adoption agency had claimed that Stefan had been taught some English, but David had yet to see evidence of it. David continued to speak, positive his son would understand his tone even if he couldn't grasp the words. "This is her maiden voyage. Her first trip, just like this is our first trip, and that makes it special." He motioned toward the stage that had been set up on the pier beneath the ship's bow. "That's why everyone's celebrating."

The ship's official christening ceremony had been held the day before and had been a closed affair, with only the cruise-line executives and VIP guests invited, but the stage hadn't yet been disassembled. Banners bearing the blue and white of the Greek flag of the ship's owner, as well as the Liberty circle of stars logo, draped the edges of the platform. In the center, a group of musicians and a dance troupe dressed in traditional white folk costumes performed for the benefit of the *Alexandra's Dream*'s first passengers. Their audience was in a festive mood, snapping their fingers in time to the music while the dancers twirled and wove through their steps.

David bobbed his head to the rhythm of the mandolins. They were playing a folk tune that seemed vaguely familiar, possibly from a movie he'd seen. He hummed a few notes. "Catchy melody, isn't it?"

Stefan turned his gaze on David. His eyes were a striking shade of blue, as cool and pale as a winter horizon and far too solemn for a child not yet five. Still, the smile that hovered at the corners of his mouth persisted. He moved his head with the music, mirroring David's motion.

David gave a silent cheer at the interaction. Hopefully, this cruise would provide countless opportunities for more. "Hey, good for you," he said. "Do you like the music?"

The child's eyes sparked. He withdrew his thumb with a pop. *"Moozika!"*

"Music. Right!" David held out his hand. "Come on, let's go closer so we can watch the dancers."

Stefan grasped David's hand quickly, as if he feared it would be withdrawn. In an instant his budding smile was replaced by a look close to panic.

Did he remember the car accident that had killed his parents? It would be a mercy if he didn't. As far as David knew, Stefan had never spoken of it to anyone. Whatever he had seen had made him run so far from the crash that the police hadn't found him until the next day. The event had traumatized him to the extent that he hadn't uttered a word until his fifth week at the orphanage. Even now he seldom talked.

David sat back on his heels and brushed the hair from Stefan's forehead. That solemn, too-old gaze locked with his, and for an instant, David felt as if he looked back in time at an image of himself thirty years ago.

He didn't need to speak the same language to understand exactly how this boy felt. He knew what it meant to be alone and powerless among strangers, trying to be brave and tough but wishing with every fiber of his being for a place to belong, to be safe, and most of all for someone to love him….

He knew in his heart he would be a good parent to Stefan. It was why he had never considered halting the adoption process after Ellie had left him. He hadn't balked when he'd learned of the recent claim by Stefan's spinster aunt, either; the absentee relative had shown up too late for her case to be considered. The adoption was meant to be. He and this child already shared a bond that went deeper than paperwork or legalities.

A seagull screeched overhead, making Stefan start and press closer to David.

"That's my boy," David murmured. He swallowed hard, struck by the simple truth of what he had just said.

That's my boy.

"I CAN'T BE PATIENT, RUDOLPH. I'm not going to stand by and watch my nephew get ripped from his country and his roots to live on the other side of the world."

Rudolph hissed out a slow breath. "Marina, I don't like the sound of that. What are you planning?"

"I'm going to talk some sense into this American kidnapper."

"No. Absolutely not. No offence, but diplomacy is not your strong suit."

"Diplomacy be damned. Their ship's due to sail at five o'clock."

"Then you wouldn't have an opportunity to speak with him even if his lawyer agreed to a meeting."

"I'll have ten days of opportunities, Rudolph, since I plan to be on board that ship."

* * * * *

Follow Marina and David as they join forces to uncover the reason behind little Stefan's unusual silence, and the secret behind the death of his parents....

Look for From Russia, With Love by Ingrid Weaver in stores June 2007.

Silhouette®
ROMANTIC
SUSPENSE

Sparked by Danger,
Fueled by Passion.

**This month and every month look for
four new heart-racing romances
set against a backdrop of suspense!**

Available in June 2007

Shelter from the Storm
by RaeAnne Thayne

A Little Bit Guilty
(Midnight Secrets miniseries)
by Jenna Mills

Mob Mistress
by Sheri WhiteFeather

A Serial Affair
by Natalie Dunbar

Available wherever you buy books!

SRS0507

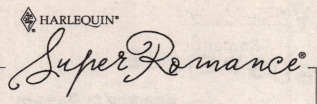

HARLEQUIN®
Super Romance®

Acclaimed author
Brenda Novak
returns to Dundee, Idaho, with

COULDA BEEN A COWBOY

After gaining custody of his infant son,
professional athlete Tyson Garnier hopes to escape
the media and find some privacy in Dundee, Idaho.
He also finds Dakota Brown. But is she ready for the
potential drama that comes with him?

Also watch for:

BLAME IT ON THE DOG by Amy Frazier
(Singles...with Kids)

HIS PERFECT WOMAN by Kay Stockham

DAD FOR LIFE by Helen Brenna
(A Little Secret)

MR. IRRESISTIBLE by Karina Bliss

WANTED MAN by Ellen K. Hartman

Available June 2007 wherever Harlequin books are sold!

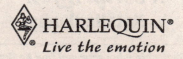

HARLEQUIN®
Live the emotion

SPECIAL EDITION™

COMING IN JUNE

HER LAST FIRST DATE

by *USA TODAY* bestsellling author
SUSAN MALLERY

After one too many bad dates, Crissy Phillips
finally swore off men. Recently widowed,
pediatrician Josh Daniels can't risk losing his
heart. With an intense attraction pulling them
together, will their fear keep them apart?
Or will one wild night change everything...?

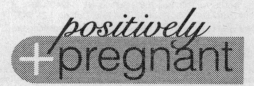

**Sometimes the unexpected
is the best news of all....**

REQUEST YOUR FREE BOOKS!
2 FREE NOVELS PLUS 2 FREE GIFTS!

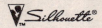

SPECIAL EDITION®
Life, Love and Family!

YES! Please send me 2 FREE Silhouette Special Edition® novels and my 2 FREE gifts. After receiving them, if I don't wish to receive any more books, I can return the shipping statement marked "cancel." If I don't cancel, I will receive 6 brand-new novels every month and be billed just $4.24 per book in the U.S., or $4.99 per book in Canada, plus 25¢ shipping and handling per book and applicable taxes, if any*. That's a savings of at least 15% off the cover price! I understand that accepting the 2 free books and gifts places me under no obligation to buy anything. I can always return a shipment and cancel at any time. Even if I never buy another book from Silhouette, the two free books and gifts are mine to keep forever.

235 SDN EEYU   335 SDN EEY6

Name	(PLEASE PRINT)
Address	Apt.
City	State/Prov.	Zip/Postal Code

Signature (if under 18, a parent or guardian must sign)

Mail to the **Silhouette Reader Service™:**
IN U.S.A.: P.O. Box 1867, Buffalo, NY 14240-1867
IN CANADA: P.O. Box 609, Fort Erie, Ontario L2A 5X3
Not valid to current Silhouette Special Edition subscribers.

Want to try two free books from another line?
Call 1-800-873-8635 or visit www.morefreebooks.com.

* Terms and prices subject to change without notice. NY residents add applicable sales tax. Canadian residents will be charged applicable provincial taxes and GST. This offer is limited to one order per household. All orders subject to approval. Credit or debit balances in a customer's account(s) may be offset by any other outstanding balance owed by or to the customer. Please allow 4 to 6 weeks for delivery.

Your Privacy: Silhouette is committed to protecting your privacy. Our Privacy Policy is available online at www.eHarlequin.com or upon request from the Reader Service. From time to time we make our lists of customers available to reputable firms who may have a product or service of interest to you. If you would prefer we not share your name and address, please check here. ☐

SSE07

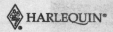

INTRIGUE

ARE YOU AFRAID OF THE DARK?

The eerie text message was only part of a night to remember for security ace Shane Peters—one minute he was dancing with Princess Ariana LeBron, holding her in his arms at a soiree of world leaders, the next he was fighting for their lives when a blackout struck and gunmen held them hostage. Their demands were simple: give them the princess.

Part of a new miniseries:

LIGHTS OUT

ROYAL LOCKDOWN

BY RUTH GLICK
WRITING AS
REBECCA YORK

On sale June 2007.

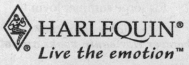

HARLEQUIN®
Live the emotion™

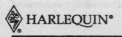

HARLEQUIN®

American ROMANCE®

is proud to present a special treat this
Fourth of July with three stories
to kick off your summer!

SUMMER LOVIN'
by
**Marin Thomas,
Laura Marie Altom
Ann Roth**

This year, celebrating the Fourth of July in Silver Cliff,
Colorado, is going to be special. There's an all-year
high school reunion taking place before the old
school building gets torn down. As old flames find
each other and new romances begin, this small
town is looking like the perfect place
for some summer lovin'!

*Available June 2007
wherever Harlequin books are sold.*